THE
SUPER KID

WITH SUPERNATURAL POWERS

P. V. George

Become
Shakespeare
.com

First published in 2018 by

Becomeshakespeare.com

Wordit Content Design & Editing Services Pvt Ltd
Unit- 26, Building A-1, Nr Wadala RTO,
Wadala (East), Mumbai 400037, India
T: +918080226699

Wordit Art Fund helps deserving authors publish their work by
providing monetary support. To apply for funding, please visit us at
www.BecomeShakespeare.com

Disclaimer

This is a work of fiction. Names, characters, events and incidents are
either the products of the author's imagination or used in a fictitious
manner. Any resemblance to actual persons, living or dead, or actual
events is purely coincidental.

©

ISBN - 978-93-88081-61-0

Also by the same author

Skits for various occasions
Moolya malurukal (Malayalam)

Dedication

To all my young readers of this book

Acknowledgement

There is quite a long list of those who deserve due commendation and my most sincere gratitude:

First and foremost, I thank the Almighty God for helping me to turn my long cherished dream of penning this novel, into a reality.

I am grateful to the Leadstart Publishers, especially Celestine Chua and Malini Nair, for going through my manuscript and then introducing me to Become Shakespeare Publication.

I do acknowledge my gratitude to Pritesh Chavan of Wordlit Art Fund for the project grant.

I am indebted to the team of Become Shakespeare Publishers (especially Pooja Dutt and Sameer Ambildhok, the Project Manager) for guiding me through the publication process and finally publishing the book in an attractive manner.

I would like to express my most sincere and heartfelt thanks to my friend, Mr. Sriram Rammohan, Coordinator Vetnet at Don Bosco ITI, Chinchwad,

Pune, Maharashtra, for editing and proof reading my book and making valuable suggestions. In spite of his busy schedule, he obliged me to do the tedious job and I do appreciate his goodwill and thank him from the bottom of my heart.

I owe huge thanks to all the readers of this book; the success of the book is in your hands. With your support I look forward to writing the sequels soon.

Contents

1. Jim runs away from his home 11

2. Jim's encounter with a Supernatural Being 23

3. Jim finds a home for himself. 27

4. Jim joins a new school 32

5. Jim's first mission as Super Kid 42

6. Cheer up India club is formed 47

7. An adulterated milk seller is punished 57

8. Chakrapani's criminal career 63

9. Seby tries to escape 69

10. Super Kid busts a criminal conspiracy 75

11. Seby's reunion with his family 83

12. Super Kid tackles two naughty boys 88

13. An ideal principal 93

14. Escape of Chakrapani and his gang 102

15. Chakrapani's hide-out in the jungle 106

16. Veeru Dada's attempts to be a Don 111

17. A bank robbery 120

18. Jim visits his family secretly 129

19. Super Kid in Stephen's office 134

20. Super Kid investigates a murder mystery 140

21. Stephen's encounter with the 'ghost of Vincent' ... 144

22. Super Kid teaches John a lesson 148

23. A chase 155

24. Veeru Dada learns the identity of Super Kid 161

25. Jim and Super Kid found missing! 170

26. Attempts to recapture Chakrapani 174

27. The three secrets 186

28. Super Kid surveys Chakrapani's hide-out 194

29. Veeru Dada's encounter with Stephen 199

30. A dead man becomes alive! 203

31. The mystery of the 'special prisoner' 209

32. A family reunion 216

33. Stephen's encounter with the 'stranger' 223

34. SP Vikram captures a dreaded Don 226

35. Super Kid's noble mission to continue 232

Jim runs away from his home

It was a chilly winter morning. Jim, a kid of just twelve, looked out through the window to have a *glimpse* outside.

He *gazed* at the horizon. The sun had not yet emerged in the sky. A thin layer of mist had *engulfed* the entire area. Still he could see night dews shining like pearls, making plants glisten. Birds chirped to each other in chorus, singing a soothing, *melodious* tune, announcing the *herald* of another new day. The morning glory with its *tranquility* was very refreshing.

A little far away, a dog barked and a *rooster* crowed. The stillness of the early morning was restored again. He was *engrossed* in the morning *serenity.*

He saw boys dropping newspapers at the doors and milkmen supplying milk. *Hawkers* started shouting to sell their goods. Morning *chorus* had begun.

"Get up, you lazy creature! Go and fetch some milk," his 'stepmother' shouted from her bed room. Her unpleasant screaming *marred* the morning stillness and the peace which he had been enjoying till then.

Jim knew that she would be sleeping under the quilt for another half an hour, at least. He was the only one awake in the whole house!

The first thing he did was to kneel down and pray to God, offering the day's activities and asking the Lord's blessing! Then he covered himself with a torn shawl and opened the door. As he stepped outside, he began to shiver with cold. An extremely cold wind was blowing, which was piercing. His hands and feet were *benumbed* with cold.

By the time he came back, the sun was just peeking out of the horizon among the mountains and its brilliant rays began shining brightly. The warm orange glow of the sun's rays had chased the mist away.

When he brought milk from the booth, his younger sister, Jane, had got ready to go to the school. He boiled some milk and gave to her.

Both were very fond of each other. As she waved her hands and walked *briskly*, bitter memories *tormented* him and Jim wiped his tears with his hands and heaved a sigh.

Jim went down his memory lane. Last year Jane was nine years old and she was studying in the fourth standard. Jim was eleven and was in the sixth standard then and he was the cleverest child in his class and also the teacher's favourite one. He was an all-rounder, exceptionally clever in studies, good at sports and cultural activities, an excellent artist and a computer expert, in short a whiz kid, rather a child *prodigy*! He had won the hearts of his companions by his gentle dealing and helping nature. He used to help his classmates who were weak in studies.

When the postman brought his report card, his joy knew no bounds. He was not only the topper in his class, but also in the whole school! His class teacher had mentioned the same on his report card. As a compliment, she had drawn two stars and a smiling face on the report card! How happy his real parents would have been seeing his performance, if they were to be alive, he thought.

With excitement and a sense of fulfillment, he showed the result to his step-father.

"Okay, okay! Now it's enough of your studies. We want you to stay back home and help us in the household work!" His stepfather, Stephen, was firm.

Jim was *stunned*. He couldn't believe his ears.

"We can't spend money for your education. We don't expect you to work later on in an office and earn", his 'step mother' added with a *scorn*. "You will help me in the kitchen and your father in the office, cleaning, buying stationery etc. Let John go for further studies and take care of the company in the future."

John was their only son. Tears welled up in Jim's eyes. Jane too started weeping bitterly. Both used to go to the school together. After that fatal day, Jim spent several nights crying and *lamenting*. His pillow had become wet with his tears in the night.

John was weak in his studies. Though he was in the eighth, he wasn't serious about his studies at all. He was a troublemaker in the school, very rude with his 'siblings', and was envious of Jim's brilliance.

The school principal and some of the teachers pleaded with Mr. and Mrs. Stephen to continue sending Jim to the school, but in vain.

One day the principal called both the parents to her room. She told them as she leaned forward, "Look Mr. Stephen, Jim is an exceptionally brilliant child. In fact, we have very high hopes about his future. We are proud to have a child like him in our school, and we are sure he will bring glory to our school and to you as well. I'm confident that he will become a great man, one day."

"We are not interested to make Jim a great man. Our hopes are in our own son, John," Stephen told *bluntly*.

"We want Jim to help us in the household work and John to study further", Mrs. Clara Stephen added.

"You are spoiling the future of a brilliant child who is an all-rounder. In fact, you are blessed to have such a kid," the principal said. "You could be a proud parent or guardian. You are aware that John is very weak in his studies."

"Leave it madam. We have told you what's in our mind," Clara told her *resentfully*.

"I know that Jim is not your own son, that's why you are treating him thus," the Principal sat back on her chair quite disappointed. She continued, "I have heard how you ill- treat him, though the property belongs to him. Have fear of God."

"You mind your own business madam," Clara told her very rudely.

"You have no right to interfere in our family affairs," Stephen got up and so did his wife and both *slammed* the door behind them as they came out.

Now Jim watched his younger sister going to the school and he thought about the days when they were going together hand in hand, chatting, laughing, *chaffing* and *jostling*. They were the most memorable and joyful days. They were the best days! He could have been in the seventh class this year!

"Why are you still standing there and doing nothing? Come on, wash the utensils", came a shower of abuses after the scolding, as thunder follows lightning. Now that his stepmother was awake, Jim knew that she wouldn't allow him to sit down even for a little while.

With bitterness and disappointment, Jim was *immersed* in his *routine* tasks.

Down his memory lane he thought about his own parents - how affectionate and caring they were! His parents had a flourishing firm called 'Trinity Enterprises'. One day Stephen, his step father, had come to his father asking for a job. His father, a kind hearted man, readily appointed him to take care of the accounts in his company. Slowly Stephen began to show his real colours. He *forged* the company's accounts, and even began to steal money. His father came to know about it and dismissed him from the job. He challenged his father and threatened him with dire *consequences*, but his father was not afraid.

After a few days, came the most shocking news. His father was killed in a road accident!

Stephen returned with *vengeance* in his mind, forcefully married his mother, after threatening her that he would kill both her children, and became the master of the house and the company. Later on all came to know that he was already married with a woman named, Clara and also had a son, named John. Stephen had kept his first marriage a top secret.

Stephen and his first wife, Clara, were not in good terms. One day they had a terrible fight mainly because Stephen was from a very poor family who couldn't meet her growing demands. Clara wanted to enjoy life with all its comforts. One day, after the fight Clara left her husband and began to live with her own parents, along with her son, John.

A second shock came to Jim and Jane when their own mother too died in an accident! Now that Stephen had become rich, he brought his first wife, Clara, back. She was as wicked and cunning as he was! Both Jim and Jane were asked to call her 'Mom' and John 'Bhaiya' (brother), though, in fact, they had no relation with them!

"The clothes are dry. Fold them nicely and keep them in the *wardrobe*, you lazy fellow."

Clara's shouting brought his mind back to the present.

After the lunch, his step mother asked him to go to the market and purchase some vegetables. This was the chance Jim was looking for – to run away from home! He had to escape from the *torture* and later on find a way to save his sister as well.

There was another reason why he had to leave the house that day itself. Sam, their driver, was very trustworthy and was fond of both Jim and Jane. They used to call him affectionately, 'Uncle Sam'.

On the previous day Uncle Sam called Jim secretly and told him, "Dear Jim, I've a confidential thing to tell you. I overheard yesterday 'your guardians', I won't call them your parents, *conspiring* against you. They are well aware that the property and the company are in your name. As long as you are alive, they cannot take hold of them and so they are planning to get you killed. I am sorry to *scare* you, child. Run away, darling, from here tomorrow itself, at the earliest, before it is dark. Save yourself. I have only two hundred rupees with me, take the money and leave home tomorrow, without fail. I can't keep you in my family because they will find you out and you can guess what could happen."

Jim was *thunderstruck*. "How cruel they are!" Jim wiped his tears. "I am worried about my dear Jane. What will they do to her? How much worried she will be, hearing that I am missing!"

"Don't worry about her. I will take care of her. If you tell Jane that you want to go away, she won't allow you to leave without her. Before she comes back, it is better you run away. I am worried about you thinking what you will do, just a child alone, out in the vast world. But your life won't be safe here, so you must leave immediately. Many questions come to my mind - who will take care of you, where will you stay, how will you find a living?.......but remember God is with you. He will take care of you. He has a plan for you, which is for your well-being. I'll be praying for you, dear child."

Uncle Sam's words *consoled* him to some extent and he too had absolute faith in God's providence.

It was two in the afternoon. His step mother had gone to her bed for a *siesta*. He now started walking to the market, with a *resolute* mind. He had decided to escape from the cruel and unjust treatment, but his mind ached when he thought about his own dear sister, whom he loved more than himself! When she comes to know that her brother is missing, what would be her condition?

"Poor thing! Let God take care of her. Once I find a shelter and some job I can take her with me," he hoped.

He was the son of a rich man, but had to walk, while his guardians enjoyed travelling in a luxurious car! He was the victim of injustice to the core!

Though the morning was chilly, the afternoon was quite hot. He took a rickshaw to the next town and then he started to walk. After walking for a long time under the *scorching* heat of the sun, he came near a forest. Being *exhausted*, he wanted to sit under the cool shade for some time, so he went inside the forest.

Besides, he didn't want anybody to notice him that he was running away from home.

Jim always *cherished* a desire to explore all the *nooks and crannies* of this wondrous world, the master creation of the *Supreme* Artist.

He sat with the *myriad* sounds of nature, for some time. There was no shouting and yelling. He fell asleep out of sheer weariness. After a short while he was awakened by the singing of the birds.

Soon he was up to further exploring the forest. He enjoyed the blissful solitude and tranquility.

The grass was partly brown and *crispy*. He looked up and saw that the trees were skyscraper tall, which swayed in the wind. To him the huge trees with branches stretched out, looked like giants waving their hands. He could see the sun's glorious rays playing hide and seek as the leaves on the trees were swaying in the wind. He was in *awe* seeing the size and majesty of the trees. The dry twigs crunched and leaves crackled under his feet. Hares *scampered* away from him up ahead. He enjoyed the orchestra of birdsong, which was *soothing*.

Presently he came upon a jewel-blue stream, which curved gently through the forest and was splashing as it flowed through the rocks. He drank handfuls of crystal clear water, which was refreshing. Far away he noticed a waterfall. He enjoyed the silver water falling from a height, splashing around and *sparkling* in the sunlight, which looked like *glittering* pearls. He wanted to go near but soon stopped as he saw elephants bathing on the other side of the river. It was an awe inspiring sight.

He did not know how the time passed. Now he could see the bright orange glow of the setting sun on the forest *canopy*, across the stream. The *aroma* of the forest was very powerful. He plucked a few berries and they were *lush* and fruity to the tongue. Thus having relieved of hunger and thirst, onward he took his steps.

He walked slowly, pausing every few feet to scan the forest for birds and animals. He enjoyed the chirping of a rich variety of birds. He also admired the beauty of wild flowers.

He was *startled* by a rustle in the shrubbery and *instinctively stared* at the noise. He saw a snake gliding through and soon it disappeared in the bush. He stood wondering at its length. The richness of the forest was *intoxicating* enough. Walking in the lap of nature *rekindled* his spirit of exploring and adventure. What an *amazing* creation by the Super Craftsman! He recalled the lines of W. H. Davies,

"What is this life if full of care,

We have no time to stand and stare."

Jim's heart was torn apart by the thought of his loving sister. He clasped his hands in prayer, "Oh, God, help me to find shelter somewhere, but now protect me from *nocturnal* animals. Keep my little sister close to your heart, protect her and give her strength to bear my missing."

It was evening and he was alone in the forest. Surprisingly, he was not scared of the wild animals. It was as though something in the forest was *beckoning* him to venture deep into the heart of the forest! Instead of coming out of the forest, he was going further deep into the forest!

Suddenly, to his great surprise he saw a very *curious* sight – a very old and *ugly* looking woman tied to a tree, was crying bitterly!! She was in *ragged* clothes. She had *sagging* skin and *wrinkled* face. She had grey hair and there were *sores* on her body which were stinking. In short, she presented a *disgusting* sight!

Moved by the *pitiable* sight, Jim rushed to her.

'What happened, granny? Who has done this to you? How come you are in the forest?"

He wiped her tears with his hands, while controlling his own. He could never stand the suffering of others.

"Untie me immediately, my child, and I will tell you my story," the old woman said in a faint voice.

"Of course, I will help you, most willingly."

After some struggle, Jim managed to release her. He helped her to stand up. The old woman thanked him *profusely*, and blessed him by laying her shaking hands on his head, "God bless you my dear child!"

As Jim gazed at her, the most astonishing thing happened! The ugly old woman disappeared and in her place stood in front of him, a fairy like figure in *dazzling* white dress! There was an unusual *splendour* and *luster* around her which lit up the dark forest. The ugly old woman had *transformed* herself into the most beautiful girl Jim had ever seen!

Jim's encounter with a supernatural being!

"WHO? Who are you?" Jim stood *awestruck* in front of her and gathered some courage to ask her.

"Don't be afraid, my dear child. I am Angel Shalom, one of the messengers of God. 'Shalom' means Peace. God has seen your miserable plight and heard your prayers. He wants to help you. Every day you make an appointment with God in the morning, don't you? God is pleased with your devotion."

Jim immediately joined his hands and knelt down with reverence. He was filled with awe.

"Am I dreaming?" wondered Jim.

"I am sent by God to choose some kind hearted persons like you to help other people in *distress*. We know that you are merciful and have a helping nature. Besides, God has seen your sad plight. I was *disguised* as an old woman to test you whether you are willing to help the people in need, that too an ugly and old person," continued the angel.

"Really? I ... I can't believe it!" Jim continued, "I am always ready to help the needy- a quality that I have *inherited* from my dear parents, but unfortunately they are no more!" His eyes were filled with tears.

"I know all about you. If you have faith in God, you are going to experience wonderful things in your further life! Your sorrow will turn into joy and you will be able to do wonderful things! Faith can even move mountains!!" the Angel smiled encouragingly.

"I do believe," Jim gathered some courage.

"I will grant you a blessing or you may call it a '*boon*' as you have read in fairy stories, by which you will be able to help anyone who is in need. But remember- never misuse it for any selfish motive, like *monetary* gain or cheap popularity. Whenever you help some people and they express gratitude to you, never take the credit for yourself but tell them that God has been gracious to them. Your aim must be to bring glory to God."

"Surely. I will give glory to God."

"The boon I am going to give you is in the form of a powerful 'thought capsule'. Whatever you think will become a reality."

Jim stood still with wondering eyes.

"You will not be bound by space and time. It implies that you can move anywhere and anytime. It's in fact, an attribute of spirits. Besides, if you want, you can be invisible to others."

"Oh, my God! That will be great. It's amazing. I'm excited."

"But you must use such divine powers only when the situation so demands. You will get these powers gradually as and when you help the people in distress."

"I'm thrilled."

"If you need my advice, think about me, and I'll appear before you and will give you counsel. Call me only when there is urgent and difficult task, not for *trifles*. When you come across someone in need of help, you may use your own *discretion* to do the needful. But if someone is not in your *vicinity* and in urgent need or panic, a message will *tickle* in your mind. Don't use your power for personal gain, but *utilize* it for the service of others. Have you got any doubts?"

"No, I have understood every word."

"Right now you need a shelter. Have absolute trust in God and He will lift you up at the right time. Don't *disclose* the divine power that you are *bestowed* upon, to anyone. Always remember not to misuse your 'boon' but to work for the glory of God – **Ad maiorem Dei gloriam,** which means all for the greater glory of God. I won't leave you, only a kid alone, just in the jungle, that too during the night. I will be with you, but you won't be able to see me, unless you so desire. May God be with you always to protect you, to guard you and to guide you!"

Suddenly the Angel and the heavenly light, which had lit the forest, *vanished* into thin air!

Now there was only cool moonlight and the light from *innumerable* stars. For a moment, Jim stood still without knowing what to do next. There was stillness as most of the animals and birds had gone to sleep. Occasionally a few nocturnal creatures made some noise.

He looked up and saw the towering trees and just thought, "The tall and huge trees look like giants waving their hands and howling!"

At once trees changed into many giants, waved their outstretched hands and shouted in a gruffly voice, "Ha! Ha! Ha!" The sound echoed in the forest!!

Immediately Jim remembered the 'thought capsule' and the words of the angel, "whatever you think will become a reality." He at once, changed his thought, "they are not giants but trees!"

Now there were no giants but tall and sturdy trees! He experienced the power of thought!

A child of his age would have been lost in the jungle, but Jim was different. Now he was not at all scared especially after the meeting with the Angel Shalom. He enjoyed an unusual peace of mind.

Then there came a tickle in his mind. He saw a family in urgent need of his help. Jim realized that it was time for him to begin his first mission as the Super Kid. By keeping absolute faith in God's mercy and in the words of His holy messenger, Jim thought in his mind, "I desire to reach a family which is in need of my help." And lo! Jim found himself in front of a house!

Jim finds a home for himself

Jim saw a family of four members, the parents and two kids, about to commit suicide by drinking poison. He wanted to know their background as what made them to take such an extreme step. No sooner did he think about their story than the entire episode was revealed to him as if in a film.

Victor, his wife Stella and two children – Jerry and Marina – formed an ideal and happy family. Victor was a practicing lawyer and stayed in a bungalow nearby. He was very honest, capable and brave.

One day, while returning home after his office hours in the late night, he saw a gang of three ruffians attacking a traveler on a bike. The man was asked to hand over his bag that contained gold and cash, which he refused. The rascals began to beat him red and blue, and the leader of the gang stabbed him. The victim was crying and was bleeding profusely.

Victor rushed there to save the victim, but to his shock he realized that the leader of the gang was none other than Anil Pandey, a criminal turned politician! Victor fought with them, but was over powered by the three. Pandey was about to *stab* Victor too, but he heard siren from a police jeep. He threatened Victor of dire consequences if he would reveal his name and report the matter to the police. Soon all of them *took to their heels*.

The victim lay unconscious. Victor called out the police, who took the victim to a well-known government hospital, but arrested Victor, accusing him of stabbing the man. Victor tried to tell the truth, but they refused to listen to him. The man was admitted in the causality, but soon died in the hospital. Victor was put in a prison.

Victor's family was shocked to hear about his plight. They were absolutely sure that he was innocent. After a few days, he was released on bail because of the influence of an advocate friend.

Pandey and his gang used to visit them and threaten to kill all of them if they would reveal their names to the police. Besides, they also demanded money to spare their lives! Now that all hopes were gone, the family had come to a *drastic* decision – ending their lives!

Victor sat dejected on a chair. His wife, Stella, was in the kitchen. The children, Jerry and Marina, were in their study room. Jerry was, twelve, and his younger sister, Marina, was ten, the same age as of Jim and Jane respectively.

Victor went to their kitchen and told his wife, "I have thought over the matter that we had discussed yesterday. Now that we don't find any way out of our problems, let us all end our lives."

"I don't know what sins we have committed because of which we have to suffer all these! Though you are innocent, all the evidences are against you. Pandey and his gang will not allow us to live in peace," Stella *sobbed* bitterly.

"When we are gone, our dear children will suffer. Who will take care of them? Let us kill all of us which may be the only solution to our suffering."

"God gave us two lovely children, but it's so sad that we are going to kill them too, though they have only started their lives! Their lives also have become miserable since the other kids call them children of a murderer!"

"I know that suicide is against God's will. But I don't find any other alternative except this extreme step! Now take this bottle of poison and mix it in the food, the last supper we are going to take together!" Tears rolled down as he said it.

As Stella took the bottle of poison, her hands shivered. Just then there was a knock at the door.

"Someone is at our door! Come on, hide the bottle somewhere as I open the door," said Victor with some anxiety. To his surprise, Victor saw Jim standing outside the door.

"Yes, child, what do you want?" Victor enquired.

"I am an orphan child and have no one to take care of me. Could you allow me to stay with you tonight?"

"We are worried about some of our grave problems. I'm very upset right now, though usually we don't turn away anyone asking for help?"

Meanwhile Stella appeared near the door and she too was *perplexed* seeing a small boy standing at the door.

"He has no one to take care of and he is asking whether we can give him shelter tonight." Victor explained to her.

"Such a lovely kid, I feel pity for him, but…..how can we help you, child? You don't know what we are going through. "

"Please don't *underestimate* me as I am only a child," he continued, "I know what's worrying you."

There was *resolution* in his voice which made them believe that he knew everything about them, he might have heard about them from others, they thought.

"I assure you that God will find a solution," assured Jim. Both Victor and Stella looked at each other with surprise and disbelief. They never expected such words from a kid.

"Anyway, come in child. It's very cold out there. Meet our children," Victor told and took him inside. Stella went to the study room and called the kids to meet Jim.

The three children sat together and had their meal. Victor and Stella postponed their idea of committing suicide as Jim was also with them.

The children chatted while eating, had a nice time and became friends instantly and *spontaneously*. Both Jerry and Marina shared their experience in their school and Jim got a strong desire to join a school. "The value of a thing is often realized when one loses it," Jim told in his mind. When he was deprived of opportunity to study further, all the more he *yearned* for it.

"Will I be able to study again? Who will give me admission?" Jim asked himself. "God will surely find a way," he said as he went to sleep.

Jim joins a new school

Next morning, Jim watched both the children going to school and it once again brought to him the sad memory of his own school days. As he thought about his dearest sister, his eyes became moist with tears and he wiped them without anyone noticing him.

"Can I stay with you? I will never trouble you in any way. Besides, I am ready to do any work for you." Jim told them the next day. He told his story till he left his home, but his meeting with the angel was kept confidential. They were moved by his story and allowed him to stay with them.

Jim told them, "I believe that God will help you to come out of this difficult situation." His words consoled them as they had a 'divine spell' upon them. Jim had changed their attitude by his power. They gave up the idea of committing suicide. Jim threw the bottle of poison away into a ditch.

Jim helped them in the household work, but he was treated like a member of the family and not as a servant.

Jerry and Marina returned in the evening after the school, with a lot of enthusiasm to meet their new friend. All the three played for a longer time. Jim helped both the friends to do their homework and cleared their doubts about studies. All of them soon discovered that Jim was not an ordinary child. He won their hearts.

A few days passed. The family legally adopted him as their son. One day Jim offered to go to the market to buy vegetables. While he was going, he saw an accident. A truck had hit a Honda City car from the rear. Jim realized that the truck driver had *deliberately* caused the accident. The car was smashed and the owner of the car, a man in his early forties, was thrown out of the car, and lay bleeding among the bush. The truck driver was trying to push the car down thinking that the man was inside it. His intention was to push the car down into the valley deep down, where escape was next to impossible. No one was around to take the man to a hospital.

Jim suddenly made a police siren using his power and hearing the sound, the truck driver drove away at great speed. Jim rushed to the man, and saw that the victim could die because of fatal head injury and severe bleeding. He removed his own shirt, tore it and tied on the wound. He collected the man's belonging as he heard the whining of an ambulance a bit far away. He could make use of his thought power, but preferred to take the trouble of running to the direction of the ambulance, and managed to call them to the spot where the man was lying.

The ambulance was heading towards a government hospital. The man was given immediate treatment. The director of the hospital could recognize the victim and he contacted his family members. Jim's blood matched with that of the injured man and Jim most willingly gave his blood. Arrangements were also made for more blood by the hospital. MRI showed severe head injury but expert doctors attended to him and he was discharged from the hospital.

The man, Muhammad Iqbal, who was affectionately and respectfully called by everyone as Iqbal sir, was a famous and a very wealthy businessman who was running several schools all over India. Soon the family came to know that it was Jim who was responsible for the timely help, which had saved his life. The rich man had only one son, Riaz, who was studying in the sixth.

Iqbal sir enquired about Jim and came to know from Victor that he was an 'orphan' who was adopted by him. He called up victor and expressed his desire to meet Jim and Victor. Both went to his house one day.

Iqbal sir lived in a bungalow which looked like a palace. He asked Jim a few questions and soon realized that he was an exceptionally brilliant child.

"I realize that you lost one year of yours. Don't worry my dear child. I will admit you in one of my schools and I'm sure you will get double promotion with your brilliant and outstanding performance," Iqbal sir told him with a smile.

"But he doesn't have his report card and Transfer Certificate from his previous school," Victor told him.

"Don't worry man. I'm running the school and I have influence in the Zilla Parishad. The educational officer is my class mate and a great friend. Get ready, young man, to join the school from tomorrow", Iqbal sir smiled and patted Jim affectionately.

He continued, "I owe my life to you, my dear child. You blood is running through my body." He told Jim and then turned to Victor and said: "I am not sure who tried to kill me, but if this kid hadn't come there, my dead body would have been lying in the deep valley, eaten by vultures! If he hadn't carried my suitcase with the valuables, I'd have been ruined, because it had many valuable things such as my passport, ATM card, certificates and many more documents, even cash worth lakhs! He is so honest that he didn't take a single rupee from it."

Iqbal sir turned to Jim and told him: "Whatever I offer you, is nothing in comparison with your great deed! Honesty needs to be rewarded."

"No sir, it's God's providence. He sent me at the right time. You must thank God and not me"

"You are very humble, my boy. Besides, I didn't expect such an answer just from a kid!" Iqbal sir smiled. Jim also smiled.

After thanking the *benefactor* profusely, Jim and Victor went back to their home, quite *jubilant*.

Next day was a Monday. Jim and Victor went to the new school with high expectation. He was overjoyed and marveled at seeing the new school. He read the name of the school written at the entrance of the school building. The school was called 'Green Valley English Medium School'.

The school was located on a hill station, amidst wonderful scenic beauty. The school was aptly named as Green Valley because one could see the lush meadows of the green valley stretched on one side of the school. There were spacious and well- furnished class rooms, a very large playground, Computer lab, Audio –Visual Hall, gymnasium, library with books of divergent subjects, swimming pool, a park within the school premise, play grounds, *ample* parking area, CCTV Camera, tight security and so on. In short, the school offered **a** highly effective and conducive student-centered environment for learning. The school had superb *ambience* too. Unknowingly Jim expressed a big 'WOW!'

Iqbal sir had a special room next to the Principal's room. Luckily he was in his room. Victor and Jim stood outside the room. A peon informed Iqbal sir that they had come.

"Yes, come in, both of you," sir called out from inside. "In fact, I am here especially for you today. Take your seat, Victor," Iqbal sir smiled very warmly. Jim stood nearby respectfully.

"Thank you, sir," Victor said as he sat down. "A school with such facilities may be charging very high fees, which I cannot afford."

"What! Who asked you to pay for my child?" Iqbal sir asked. "He is not only your child but mine as well. Yes, here the fees are high indeed, about a lakh per year. But I don't want any penny from him. Besides, he will surely get scholarships. Don't ever dare to insult me by talking about fees. My life is a gift given by him, man!"

"I am sorry sir. "

"That's alright. Don't take it to your heart. Jim, from tomorrow, you are going to start your studies in my school. I have already informed the principal to give you admission. Both of you go around and have a look at the school and the premises."

After thanking their benefactor profusely, they left the room and went around, saw the school campus and were thrilled by the *amenities*. Gladly and excitedly they went home.

Riaz, the only son of Iqbal sir, was very weak in his studies and hated going to school, which had worried his parents. Jim started taking up his studies and soon Riaz started liking his studies and he improved *tremendously*. Slowly he began to enjoy his studies. Iqbal sir was extremely happy and he loved Jim like his own child. He gave admission also to Jerry and Marina in his school. Riaz, Jim, Jerry and Marina became bosom friends.

Thus Jim soon found a home and he could study in the best school one could think of! He thanked God as he knew that it was all His doing.

He spent the happiest days of his life. But the thought of his sister, Jane, again worried him. Victor found him sitting troubled and asked the reason.

"The thought about my little sister, is worrying me."

'Don't worry, child. Go and bring your little sister. We will be happy to have one more daughter," Stella consoled him.

Jim asked angel Shalom's counsel whether he could bring his sister with him, which the angel allowed most willingly. Jim met his sister next day in the school. Her joy was *boundless* to see her dearest brother again. She ran to him and embraced him tightly.

"Where were you, Bhaiyya (brother)?" She asked him while tears rolling down her cheeks. "I was so much worried about you."

"I will tell you, dearest Jane. Let me first hear about you."

Jane narrated to him how she was ill-treated by the wicked step mother and others. She showed him the burning mark on her little thighs.

"They used to force me to do all kinds of work. One day I was sick and couldn't get up in the morning to wash clothes. Our wicked mom heated a piece of iron and burnt my legs. It was paining so much." Little Jane sobbed again.

"God will wipe your tears also, my dear Jane." He told how he got shelter and how he had got admission in the school. But he kept his encounter with the angel a secret.

"Our dear God cares for us. Don't worry any more. I have come to take you with me. Now come with me." Jim embraced her again warmly. Just then they saw

Uncle Sam passing by and he too was very happy to see Jim again. They went behind a tree so that John must not see them. Jim told him about his story.

"I knew that you will do well. God will not abandon a kind child like you," Uncle Sam heaved a sigh of relief. "Take Jane with you. Poor thing! How much she longed to see you!!"

Soon Jane too was admitted in the school along with Jim. Little Jane's joy knew no bounds.

Happiness doesn't last long as sadness also doesn't. Life has both these factors in different proportions. To everyone's anguish Victor got a letter from the court to appear there after two days regarding the murder case.

Victor's face turned pale as he read the letter. Jim noticed it and was pained much by the sad plight of Victor who was unusually and exceptionally good, helpful and kind.

There was a CCTV installed somewhere nearby the area where the murder had taken place. Now Jim using his divine powers, made the murder scene imprinted on the screen. The face of the murderer was clearly visible on the camera.

Next, Jim as Super Kid, told Victor that there could be proof available on the CCTV camera. Victor immediately checked the camera, found the evidence and was very happy and relieved. He went to his advocate friend and informed about the CCTV coverage. The advocate approached SP Vikram and told him about the crime and the evidence available on the CCTV. Soon Anil Pandey and his gang were caught. Super Kid using his power created a desire in Anil Pandey and his gang to confess all the crimes that they had committed. Trial procedure took place and Anil Pandey admitted that he had killed the man on a bike and that Victor was innocent. After the court procedures, the judge declared Victor innocent and that the real murderers, Anil Pandey and his gang, were to be hanged till death.

There was great joy and relief in Victor's family.

x   x   x   x

When Jane didn't return after the school, Clara became a bit disturbed and rang up to her husband, Stephen, who was still in the company.

"Jane hasn't returned from the school. You know very well that I have no concern for her but I don't want to face any possible enquiries by the police, in case something has happened to her."

"Don't worry. I think that she also has run away from home like her brother Jim had done. If that's to be true, we have easily got rid of one more nuisance," Stephen told.

"That's true. But if the class teacher asks us the reason for her absence in her class, what explanation can we give her?"

"We shall inform her that we have withdrawn the child from their school."

"The principal may call us in the office and enquire as

why we have done so, as in the case of that damn kid, Jim."

"We will tell her that we are not interested to send the child to their school any more. It's none of their business to ask for further explanations, that's all."

"If neighbours ask about her missing, we will tell them that she is sent to her relative's family. Well, she was a help in doing some household work. No problem, we can appoint a maid servant. In fact, as you said, it's good that this girl also has gone away. Now we have only our family members here."

"Yes, let us do hope that both the kids never come back again. In case they return any time, I'll send them also to be with their parents! Let all of them be together up in the heaven! Ha! Ha!!"

Stephen hanged up the phone. But both were not aware of the saying, 'man proposes but God disposes!' They did not know what was in store for them!

Jim's first mission as Super Kid

One day, to every child's excitement, School Picnic was announced by the Principal, Mrs. Susan, during the school assembly. The place chosen was a famous water park. The Children cheered and welcomed the idea. There was high voltage excitement and joy in every heart.

The children waited eagerly for the weekend to arrive, to go for the much awaited picnic. The children were taken in luxury video coaches to the destination. They danced and sang songs in the bus. Jim, Jane, Jerry, Marina and Riaz sat together in the bus and enjoyed the fun.

Abu, Ravi and Tony were the most mischievous boys in the school. Abu and Tony hailed from rich families and were studying in the eighth. The parents of Abu and Tony were staying abroad. Ravi was the son of a police guard at the jail. Only a few tough teachers could tackle them in the class. They used to *turn deaf ears* to the advice given by their teachers. Often they were called to the Principal's room and were made to sit there. They were together everywhere.

As soon as the Children reached the picnic spot, some of them were taken to various rides and some others to the swimming pool. Another group enjoyed rain dance. The teachers and the principal too joined the children.

Vinay was a boy of twelve, who was suffering from *autism* and the trio, used to make fun of him. He sat on a bench alone near the swimming pool watching his class mates and others enjoying the fun. He was fat and dark, and had no attractive features. His nose was flat and there were scars and pimples on his face which made his appearance very funny.

As artificial waves were created in the swimming pool, the children shouted with merriment. They danced in the pool to the rocking music. As usual Abu, Ravi and Tony were up to some mischief. The trio came out of the Wave pool and decided to make fun of Vinay. They sat near him and started their usual *pranks*.

"Look at this fellow, how funny he looks! He *resembles* a frog!!" Abu said and all the three jeered at him.

"To my wild imagination, he looks like a young hippopotamus!" Ravi's imagination went further wild.

"I feel like comparing him with a chimpanzee! We may call him Chimpu!!" Tony added and all of them roared with laughter.

Their comments hurt Vinay to the core, but he did not utter a word. Tears welled up in his eyes.

"Let's play a game", Abu suggested. "I will give this Chimpu a nice beating on his back and will run around the swamp there. Both of you try to catch me. If you fail to catch me, I will return and hit Chimpu on the back. Then we will take turns."

"Good idea, guys!" exclaimed Ravi.

"That will be fun!" Tony agreed and winked at his friends.

Abu hit Vinay and began to run. It hurt Vinay, but he remained silent. The other two boys chased Abu. As Abu turned back to see whether his friends were near him, he accidently lost balance after his legs hit on a stone. He was thrown into the fencing but the fencing gave in. As a result he fell into the swamp with a splashing sound.

Ravi and Tony screamed aloud and hearing their cry, some of the children and teachers rushed there. They saw Abu going down the marshy land, coming up again and helplessly shouting for help. No one had the courage to jump down. Abu's class teacher sent one boy to report the matter to the principal, and another one to call the security.

Everyone was looking at Abu's plight and there was fear and panic in every eye. The swamp was quite deep. There was a warning board placed near the swamp to caution not to go near the swamp. The trio had ignored the warning.

Everyone looked anxiously at the helpless boy who was struggling for his life. The child, who was sent to call the peon, came running and told the teacher that the security was not found at the gate. The

Principal too rushed to the spot, but didn't know what to do.

"SPLASH!"

The sound of water attracted every one's attention. To their astonishment, they saw Vinay diving into the swamp. Within seconds, he brought Abu near the fencing. The security guard meanwhile reached there and stretched a stick towards Abu. Abu holding the stick, tried to climb up. Vinay pushed him from down and finally Abu managed to climb up.

To every one's shock, now Vinay slipped and fell into the swamp. Water splashed around. There was horror in every eye. Vinay was about to drown in the swamp.

Jim and his friends were enjoying the rides and did not know about the incident. Suddenly there was a tickle in Jim's brain. He saw in his mind the happening at the swamp and realized that his help was urgently needed there.

Jim wished for an outfit to hide his identity as Super Kid. He thought of a white coloured robe to cover his body and a blue jacket to wear over the robe. He also wished to have a brown mask to *conceal* his face. To him white symbolized purity of mind and blue represented the sky or heaven which is believed to be God's abode. Brown stood for the soil of the earth, his earthly life. And lo, as soon as he thought about them, he got dressed up in the same way as he had wished for! At once he reached the spot. He dived into the swamp and brought Vinay safely. All were astonished seeing Super Kid appearing from nowhere.

"Who are you, kid?" The Principal asked him with awe.

"You may call me Super Kid. I am an ambassador of God, sent by Him to help those in distress", Jim told her. None could see the face of Jim clearly as it was covered by the mask - like *outfit*.

"Thank you immensely for saving him," the principal told him with disbelief.

"Thank God and all glory to Him alone," Jim told everyone. He pointed at Ravi, Tony and Abu and continued, "These boys used to make fun of Vinay's deformities, but it was Vinay who had saved Abu from drowning. I do appreciate Vinay's daring noble deed! Never make fun of people having shortcomings. It hurts not only the person who is targeted but also makes God, the Creator, sad!"

Having finished saying this, Super Kid disappeared suddenly. All stood wondering at the unusual happening.

6

Cheer up India club is formed

All who were present at the picnic spot looked at each other in awe and *bewilderment*. There was fear and wonder in everyone's mind. All started to talk about Super Kid and wondered at his sudden appearance.

Abu was moved by remorse and was ashamed of his own behaviour. The noble act of Vinay had touched Ravi and Tony as well. Abu got up and touched Vinay's feet and asked for his forgiveness. There were tears in his eyes which showed that he was serious about his repentance.

"Don't worry, Abu. I'm happy to notice that you have changed and that makes me happy," Vinay lifted Abu and hugged him. Everyone clapped.

The principal was watching the boys. She patted Vinay and appreciated him, "I am proud of you, dear child, rather, the whole school salutes your bravery and the noblest gesture of saving your classmate at the risk of your own life! I will recommend your name for a bravery award!!"

"No madam, I do not expect any reward for my deed. I only wanted to save a life that was in danger."

"Don't say 'no', dear. You deserve appreciation and that will set an example for others to *emulate.'*

Vinay agreed. Everyone clapped again.

The principal *looked daggers at* Abu, Ravi and Tony. She warned them, "Now you naughtiest ones, I do hope that this incident has opened your eyes and you will not do any more mischief. We all want to see you behave better. I will deal with you all very sternly if I find anyone teasing and making fun of others."

Jim and his friends continued playing in the water. Jim's friends came to know about the happenings only when they had gathered to get into the bus. The Principal addressed everyone and narrated the incident.

The next day, during the assembly, the Principal addressed the students and briefed about the incident. Iqbal sir also was present on the occasion and appreciated Vinay's noble deed and gave a cash award to him.

Jim welcomed Vinay also in his friends circle and other friends too agreed to Jim's decision. Jim took up helping Vinay in his studies voluntarily and the boy began to show remarkable improvement.

After the incident, the parents of both Abu and Tony took them to Dubai where they were staying. The children were sent to a school there. The three friends were very sad. Ravi also joined Jim's friends- circle.

Thus now their friends circle expanded into a group of seven children - Jim, Jane, Jerry, Marina, Riaz, Vinay and Ravi.

The group expressed a desire to form a Social Service Club to help the needy ones. It was Jim's idea and others supported it most willingly. They thought about a name for it – 'Cheer up India club'. The motive was to spread cheer in the unfortunate and the needy ones. They went to the principal and expressed their plan. The principal, Mrs. Susan, most happily welcomed the idea and offered her full support to it. She was the first one to contribute to it. At Jim's request, Iqbal sir offered three lakhs most willingly!

As days passed more and more students joined the group. The Supervisor of the school, Richard sir, was a very dedicated man who was also interested in charity work. He was made the Captain of the Cheer up India club. Under his able guidance the children began to collect grains, pulses, cereals, old clothes, articles, and even cash from the children and from those who were willing to contribute towards the noble cause. Soon they could raise a very large fund.

The members of the Cheer up India club sacrificed their pocket money or some of their favourite dishes and contributed the amount towards the noble cause. The fund was used for the needy. Under the leadership of Jim, the members of the club planned a cleanliness drive in the slums and Railway station platforms. The group met the school principal, Susan, who readily appreciated and encouraged the members of the club and gave green signal to go ahead with their programme. She informed the director, Iqbal sir, who also was very much pleased with the idea and gave *blanket permission* to them. He promised them that he would obtain necessary permission from the police officer.

During the assembly, the Principal announced details of the programme. The Campaign was planned out to be held on a weekend. The student body along with the Principal and the Supervisor chalked out details of the programme.

'The Cheer up India' team was very excited as the day *dawned*. The stage was well decorated in a befitting manner. Jim and a few other children prepared attractive and striking backdrops, which contained captivating slogans like, 'Cleanliness is next to godliness', 'Clean India is healthy India', "We did not inherit the earth from our ancestors; we have borrowed it from our children" 'Be alert about dirt', 'Clean India – Green India – Cheer up India' etc.

The corporator of the area was the chief guest.

After welcoming and introducing the chief guest, the Principal gave necessary instructions about the cleanliness drive. She said proudly," I am happy that the children under the leadership of Jim have come forward expressing their interest in participating the honourable Prime Minister's clarion call to 'Swatch Bharat Abhiyan' (Clean India Campaign) by cleaning the school premises and some of the slum areas and saying 'no' to plastics. Plastic is a non- bio degradable substance which is harmful and pollute the environment. They choke up the drainage and cause flood. So let us co-operate with the government and say 'no' to the usage of plastic. Let us join our hands together to build a clean India. Let us spread cheer among the people, especially the marginalized poor, through 'Cheer up India's activities!"

The Corporator in his speech said, "The noble work that your school has taken up is really praiseworthy. Plastic pollution contaminates our environment and creates many grave environmental problems. If plastics are burnt, they can infuse the air with toxic elements which in turn cause serious health issues. Polythene bags are responsible for clogging of drainage system which can cause flood. When plastics are eaten accidently by animals, they can block their digestive tract and can cause their death. We are inviting health hazards by not keeping our environment clean. So it is imperative to take up various campaigns and spread the message of creating a clean and green India. It is very heartening to find school children, the future citizens of our country, are aware of these facts and that they have taken initiative to keep the surrounding clean. I do appreciate the school management and the children for such noble efforts. I hope that other schools across the country also emulate the noble examples set by the Green Valley School. Hats off to Cheer up India!"

A thundering applause followed his speech. Some of the children were encouraged to give *extempore* speeches.

The children from the seventh to ninth classes were divided into different groups who undertook the cleanliness drive under the guidance of their class teachers and subject teachers. The corporator and the Principal also participated in the Campaign. All wore white coloured caps with the caption Cheer up India club printed on them. They picked up plastic items littered on the streets, lanes and railway platforms. They collected them in bags made of cloth. All were given gloves to keep themselves protected from germs.

As the children went around cleaning the area by picking up the litters and sweeping, some of the people in the slum made fun of them. As a few children reached a hut to sweep the premises, a door was flung open suddenly and out came an evil looking man about six feet tall and well-built. He had a thick moustache with its both edges twisted and turned upwards. His bloodshot eyes stared at the children angrily. He shouted at the children, "Who told you to clean this area? Go away from here at once!"

His evil looking appearance and the *husky* voice made the children scared and they ran away. Seeing them fleeing, some of the children from the slum clapped and enjoyed the fun.

Hearing the noise outside two more tough looking men also came out and watched the children running away.

Richard sir, the Supervisor, noticed some of the children running as if frightened. He stopped them and enquired, "What happened, children? Why are you running away so fast?"

"There's a terrible looking man over there who shouted at us to go from here," one of the boys said while casting his eyes towards the hut.

"Don't worry. Come with me."

The children followed sir and approached the hut where the stranger was still standing. His companions also were standing with him staring at the children.

"Why did you shout at our children? We have come here to clean your area, in fact you should be happy about it," sir told him.

"We don't want anybody to clean here. We can take care of our area."

"We have planned this cleaning drive to make our children aware of the value of social service and the need for cleanliness. We have only noble intention."

"Did we ask you to do social service here? Hey master, you do your teaching and don't interfere in our lives."

He then turned towards the children and asked *tauntingly,* "Are you sent to the school to learn or to sweep the streets? Don't listen to your silly master and waste your time!"

"Our children know very well whom to listen. We have no intention to disturb you in any way. I don't understand why you get angry at us?"

"Our boss doesn't like anybody questioning him. Do you understand master?" One of the gangsters asked angrily.

"We don't like anybody interfering in our lives," the other one added.

"Now get out from here, I won't allow you to remain here any longer," the leader of the group shouted in a threatening tone.

Then he took two steps forward and pushed Richard sir. Sir lost his balance, but an elderly man at once came forward and held sir's hand. He whispered in his ears, "He is called Veeru Dada, a dreaded underworld don. The other two are his companions who are also evil people. You better go away from here."

"Thank you, uncle. You held my hand; otherwise I would have fallen down."

Jim got a tickling and suddenly appeared as Super Kid on the scene with a *baton*. The children were excited to see him. The villagers and the children from the slum were astonished to see him.

"I am known as Super Kid. My mission is to help the needy and prevent wicked people from troubling others."

"Super Kid, BAH! Who believes in such nonsense? Get out from here!" Veeru Dada shouted.

"You don't understand mild language. I have bought a baton which will teach you a lesson not to trouble people doing good work."

Super Kid sent his baton to teach a lesson to Veeru Dada, his companions and also those kids who had jeered at them. The baton thrashed them mercilessly.

People watched it wondering at the happening and then enjoyed the fun. Looking at their plight everyone agreed that those 'undesirable elements' in the society deserved such treatment.

Veeru Dada and his companions had selfish motive to prevent the cleanliness drive as they were involved in criminal activities and the slum was one of their hide-outs. They feared that the activities of the 'Cheer up India' might attract the attention of the police.

Veeru Dada writhed in pain and *gnashed* his teeth in anger.

"You a mere kid in a 'fancy dress', how dare to beat me? I will show you who I am!"

Veeru Dada suddenly ran inside his hut, came out holding a knife and rushed at Super kid. He lifted his knife to stab Super Kid. At once the knife became boiling hot and the Don threw it away instantly.

"Are you a magician? I......I can't believe it!"

He bent down to pick up the knife, but the knife was not seen at all!

"Where is my knife? What's happening?"

Super Kid's baton continued thrashing the criminals severely. Finally Veeru Dada joined his hands and cried, "Please stop. I can't bear it any longer. Let the children clean or do whatever they want."

The criminals sat down completely exhausted.

Now the children continued their cleanliness drive

in the slum without any hindrance. The children felt a kind of great satisfaction that they had done something for the welfare of the society. They realized that real education is not just confined to the bookish knowledge, but it must include civic sense and awareness about the needy in the society as well.

The newspapers covered the news and the message was sent across the length and breadth of the country. India was waking up. Super Kid became a topic of discussion everywhere.

After the examination, the Cheer up India club took up another campaign, spreading literacy. A few children visited some of the slum areas and started educating the children, who were not sent to school. The school held literacy classes for the illiterate adults during the vacation. Jim and other children volunteered to take classes for them.

The club again raised fund to help the needy. The school was slowly turning into a social service centre *catering to* the needs of not only the children but also the society at large. 'Cheer up India' had become a huge success.

In another drive, the Cheer up India club signed a memorandum to the Corporation requesting the authorities to build houses for the slum dwellers and to take action on the people who *defecate* on the roads and in the public places. They also sent a copy to the local police station and waited for the implementation of their proposals.

7

An adulterated milk seller is punished

Rokade, was a tall and broad shouldered villager who earned his living by selling milk. He owned two cows and two buffaloes. People knew that he sold *adulterated* milk, but they had no other source where they could buy milk. The milk that he sold contained more water than milk. He earned a lot of money by his *malpractice*.

One day, Jim, Jane, Jerry and Marina went for a walk through a jungle. When they came near a river, they saw Rokade filling his milk can with water from the river.

"Hey, uncle, why are you adding river water to the milk?' Jim asked Rokade.

"Who are you to question me? Go away!" Rokade screamed angrily.

"The water is not at all clean. Women wash their clothes, some people clean their animals and some others take bath," Jerry added.

"Uncle, you are doing something wrong. Even babies are given this milk. They may fall sick." Jane said.

"It's not my concern to worry about the health of the people. My business is selling milk and earning money. If people don't fall sick how will the doctors earn their money? In that sense, I am doing a social work!" Rokade laughed at his own joke. "You, kids, better mind your own business, otherwise I will flog you. You don't know Rokade."

By now Rokade filled his can with water and closed it.

"But even by selling pure milk, you can earn enough. Why to add water to milk?" Jane questioned him.

"That's because I want to earn more money, just simple as that, you little silly girl. Actually I'm not adding water to milk but milk to water!" Rokade chuckled and tapped on her shoulders.

"We will tell the people that you sell milk with contaminated water from the river. Then they will stop buying milk from you," Jerry told him as Rokade was getting ready to go away.

"How dare you threaten me, you silly *brats*? I'm made of a very tough material. Don't dare to talk to me like this. Just shut up your mouth and mind your own business."

"Only Super Kid can teach this guy a lesson," Jane said hopefully.

"But where to find him?" asked Jerry.

"He may be watching us from somewhere." Jim said innocently.

"Super Kid? Who is this *clown*? Has he got super power?" Rokade made fun of them.

"You will realize it if you meet him. He will *thrash* you with his baton," Jerry said with a smile.

Rokade was half mad with rage, *grabbed* a stick lying there and raised it to beat them.

Jim acted suddenly. He stayed with the other children but his other self, Super Kid appeared there from nowhere. The kids were excited to see him.

The stick in Rokade's hand turned a snake and it made a hissing sound. Rokade was shocked and *appalled*. He threw it away instantly.

The cobra raised its head and stood in front of him about to attack him. Rokade began to run around the kids. "Hey, Ram. Save me," he *yelled* as he ran. One of the cans fell from his hand, the lid opened and the adulterated milk *spilled* on the ground.

The children laughed seeing his *plight*. After some time the snake vanished and Rokade heaved a sigh of relief. Seeing the loss of milk, he became *desperate* and half mad.

"Who are you kid, in that funny dress?" Rokade asked while panting for breath. "How did the stick suddenly turn into a cobra? Are you a magician?" A cold *shudder* ran through him.

"How dare you behave so roughly with these kids?

You wanted to beat the children, didn't you? Now you taste some beatings!" Super Kid told him.

Suddenly the same stick, which Rokade had used to beat the kids, appeared in front of him and it began to shower beatings on Rokade. He ran here and there, screaming.

"Stop beating me. Who are you?" Rokade, with perspiration streaming down his face, asked *banteringly*.

"People call me Super Kid. I help the needy and punish the guilty. That's my mission."

"Stop *thrashing* me, I can't bear it any longer. I'll go mad."

"Now if you want me to stop beating you, promise me that you will stop your malpractice of selling adulterated milk. You will sell only pure milk. "

"Please stop the baton. Let me speak."

The stick disappeared and Rokade sat down exhausted, grasping for breath.

"Why should I stop adding water to milk? I have been doing it for the past twenty years. No one dared to question me thus." After mustering some courage Rokade said while looking around to check whether the baton was seen somewhere. There was terror in his eyes but *arrogance* in his words.

"Now I'm here daring to question you and to stop you from doing such wrong things. You can't charge people for the water you add to the milk. Hereafter you are going to sell only pure milk and charge for the same."

"You look like a kid, though I can't see you properly in that funny dress. How can you command me?"

"After getting so many beatings, you are the same, an arrogant and ill -mannered guy. You haven't learnt a lesson. Take some more."

Suddenly the baton appeared again and it moved with lightning speed. Rokade cried like a child and tried to catch hold of the baton, but in vain. The children laughed and clapped their hands seeing the plight of the villainous character, which was extremely annoying to Rokade.

"Please stop. I can't stand it any longer."

Super Kid stopped beating.

"Now are you ready to promise me that you will stop your malpractice?"

"I'm ready for anything, but please stop the beatings."

"Now ask pardon from the people for cheating them for such a long time."

"No, I won't"

"Ok, let the baton do its work."

The baton appeared again *hurled* around him menacingly.

"Okay, okay. No more thrashing. I'll do whatever you tell me."

"Now do you want to see how much water you have added in the milk? Look into your milk can."

As he looked into the can which was filled to its brim, the level of the milk lowered and lo! Only less than half of the can contained milk. The milk was thick and pure.

"Hey, where did the milk disappear?" Rokade asked with shock and surprise.

"Milk didn't disappear, only the water! Hereafter you are going to charge only half the price for the milk. You must sell only pure milk from today. You need to *compensate* for the loss the people have been suffering owing to buying adulterated milk from you."

"It will be great loss for me, but still I have to listen to you. I don't want any more those damn beatings with your baton!"

"Anytime you happen to forget what I've told you, remember the baton. You will be inviting it!"

"I'll neither forget you nor the baton!"

"That's good! Remember, wealth earned through evil ways, will not last longer. If God allows you to fall sick, you may have to shell out much more than what you have earned through unfair means."

Super Kid *vanished* suddenly. Rokade stood still for some time wondering whether what he had been going through was a dream or reality.

Chakrapani's criminal 'career'

Chakrapani began his criminal 'career' in a small way as the *adage* goes, 'the beginning of all things are small'. He entered into a criminal circle with petty thefts. He was caught and punished often, but he preferred to grow from bad to worse. His father, a labourer in a factory, was a drunkard who *seldom* cared for his family. He spent most part of his wages for buying liquor. His wife ran the family by doing household works in a few families.

Chakrapani had studied only up to fourth class; the reasons were his lack of interest on one hand and the family's poor background, on the other. In fact, he was dismissed from the school for stealing tiffin, pens etc. of his companions. All efforts to mend his ways turned futile, and the school authorities finally decided to get rid of him.

Chakrapani later on grew up not only physically but also in his criminal activities. He ran a racket for pick pocketing using mostly young children from the slum areas. He even kidnapped children from well to do families and turned them into criminals. He personally trained them and now became a don, dreaded by the people in and around the area.

He had many hide-outs, and he operated from different places. The police had no clue of his hide-outs.

Superintend of Police, Vikram, an efficient and honest police officer, knew about the criminal activities of Chakrapani and was always in hot pursuit of him. Having no much trust on his *subordinates*, he used to investigate most of the cases.

Chakrapani now sat on an easy chair in his hide-out while the trained young criminals were counting the day's collection.

"How much is today's collection, more or less than that of the previous days?" the Don asked in a husky voice.

"Boss, it is a record breaking collection!" said Salim, a young man in his twenties, the leader of the youngster's gang. He was jubilant about their collection. He showed a bag that contained the *booty*. Chakrapani lifted the golden chains and glanced upon the cash. But he did not join the cheer of the gang.

"Are you satisfied with this? Certainly I'm not. My aim is much higher, including looting bank, Jewelry shops, rich homes etc., do you understand, folks?" They noticed that his face was red with anger.

"How much did you collect today, Seby?" He asked one of the boys who sat in the corner, quite sad.

"I could collect only five thousand rupees today. I was not keeping well, Boss." Seby was very scared of the Don and in fact, it was against his will to plunder and to lead a life with looted wealth. He was kidnapped from a good family two years ago, and trained to steal from the rich. When he was staying with his family he was taught that it was a great sin to steal. He was put into severe torture and was finally forced into the present undesirable life style! He always longed to escape from the clutches of the Don and to join back his family.

"Oh, I see. Were you really sick or trying to *bluff* me? You know very well that I've no soft corner at all, my heart is the heart of a hardcore criminal and I'm proud to be so. I expect that all of you harden yours too! Now all of you know that when someone brings very meager loot, what's his fate, don't you, guys?"

"Yes, Boss," others answered in a chorus.

"So, you stay hungry for two days. No one will give him anything, do you understand? If anyone disobeys me or tries to escape from here, his fate is boiled water shower! Ha! Ha!!" He roared with a devilish laughter. "And if any one dreams to betray me, he will not live to see the next day!" To Seby, he looked like a real devil in a human form!

Seby knew very well that there were boys in the gang like Salim, Veeru and Jacky who used to do spy work on others and report the matter to the boss. Escape from there was like a distant dream!

"Now, let us plan as how to expand our team further

and how to increase the amount of our booty." The Don looked for some practical suggestions.

"I think the best idea is to sell drugs in the schools and colleges," Salim suggested.

"We may kidnap children from rich families and ask for ransom," Veeru suggested.

"We can loot also petrol pumps and even hospitals," Jackey smiled.

"And what do you suggest, Seby? Are you *at the end of your wits*?" the Don jeered at him. He always took pleasure in taunting him.

Seby kept mum.

"Come on, you dirty pig, good for nothing fellow, speak up, I say."

"I don't know, Boss. I am feeling giddiness. I've temperature, too. Can I go to bed?"

"Veeru, check him whether he is telling the truth?"

Veeru put his hand on the forehead of Seby and said, "Yes, Boss. He has high fever."

"Ok, then, today you may go to sleep. If you are not fit, how can you do the business for me?"

Thus one more day came to an end. The next day, again there was a meeting to plan out further course of action. They planned to kidnap a child from a well-to-do family. Seby still had temperature.

"Do you know who the richest person in this area is?"

The Don asked looking at every one.

"Yes, Boss, I know very well that one Iqbal sir is running many schools like Green Valley, Rose Wood, Valley View etc. He has a flourishing business," Salim answered promptly.

"Oh, yes. I have heard about him, great idea" the Don appreciated the suggestion.

'He has a son, rather the only son. If we kidnap him, we can ask crores as ransom and his father will be too ready to give the amount," Jackey smiled.

"But much risk is involved. SP Vikram is a friend of Iqbal sir and he is always looking for us," Veeru became a little more practical.

"Yes, of course, our life is full of risks, but aren't we successful? Without daring, nothing can be achieved. I am going to involve elders also like Patel, Jaffar and Vicky Singh in this operation. Tomorrow we are going to kidnap Iqbal's son and going to demand a ransom of two crores! Two crores, ha, ha!! Why can't we be millionairs and billionairs? Let others struggle to earn money and we will loot them easily and then enjoy. Don't you like the idea? Ha! Ha!!" The Don roared again.

"What a devilish villain!" Thought Seby.

He shuddered at the thought of more kidnappings. "One more innocent child is going to be a victim of in human act. Oh, God, have mercy on the family. May this villain's evil plan become an utter failure. Let them be nabbed by the police. If only someone with super power could rescue me from this hell! Will I ever be able to meet my dad, mom and my sister? How much they miss me! They may be spending sleepless nights and weeping bitterly over my loss," Seby said in his mind desperately.

His cheeks were wet with tears. He wiped them with his hands.

He searched in the drawer of a table and found a tablet which was used to get relief from fever. With great difficulty he went to the kitchen and found some water. He swallowed the tablet and drank a glass of water.

Sam was very hungry but he knew that if he ate any food, the villain might shoot him dead!

Slowly he walked to his bed and lay down.

"Thank you God for giving me relief from the fever," he said another prayer and soon slept due to *exhaustion* and by the effect of the medicine.

9

Seby tries to escape

Seby woke up and felt much relief. The fever had gone. He looked at the clock and noticed that it was three o'clock in the morning.

He got up, went to the window and looked out.

The nature outside was bathed in full moon, which was soothing. The sky was *studded* with innumerable twinkling stars.

He just checked the door and was surprised to find that it was not locked. Someone might have forgotten, Seby thought.

He looked around and realized that nobody was awake at that time. Suddenly an idea stuck him; why not try to escape from these criminals?

He went to the door as *stealthily* as a cat, opened the door slowly, stepped out and closed the door behind. Still no one was awake!

His heart was *pounding* fast out of fear and uncertainty.

He looked around and observed some trees and bushes. The area looked very unfamiliar to him as he was always blindfolded before taken out for stealing.

There were no lights in that part of the area but he could see the surrounding in the moonlight.

Suddenly a door opened with a creaking sound behind him and instantly Seby hid behind a tree. A man got out and went to the other side for answering the nature's call.

Seby could hear the pounding of his own heart. After some time the man went in and closed the door. Seby heaved a sigh of relief.

He got up and moved slowly. Far away he could see street lights. Streets were almost vacant except for occasional plying of some trucks. Clouds hid the moon for some time.

"If I could reach the road, perhaps I could escape!" Seby thought.

As he walked, dry leaves *rustled* under his feet.

Often he looked back. To his shock, he saw two figures coming out of the door. Torch light was flashed around. Seby suddenly sat behind a bush. The figures started moving about and Seby understood that they were looking for him! He was almost frozen with fright.

As the sounds of footsteps became louder, his body started to shiver with fear.

Now the moon came out from behind a cloud and flooded its silver light. The two figures came near and he could recognize them. They were Jackey and Salim!!

The two hard core criminals flashed torchlight among the bush. At that time there was a rustling on the other side, perhaps a mouse just scampered by. Both the boys ran to the direction of the sound.

Seby got up and ran towards the street. He was running as if the devil were on his heels! He saw a truck halted there. He ran panting for breath and reached the truck. He slowly climbed the truck behind. It was empty and he lay down with exhaustion. Then slowly he got up and looked outside. He saw the driver just getting into his seat and soon he started the engine.

As the truck moved forward he saw Jackey and Salim running towards the truck at their full speed.

"Hey stop, STOP!!" One of them screamed. The driver couldn't hear them and the truck picked up speed. Sam heaved a sigh again.

His relief was short lived. He saw Jackey and Salim following the truck on a bike! The chasing took place for some time.

Soon their bike overtook the truck and stopped in the front, blocking the way.

The driver shouted at them. Keeping the bike as an *obstruction*, the boys climbed the truck and pulled Seby out.

A cold shudder ran through Seby. He trembled like rose leaves. They began to beat him severely.

The driver jumped down and came to them.

"Hey, what's going on here? Why are you beating the kid?"

Seby was about to shout. Jackey covered his mouth with one of his hands.

"Mind your own business, man. He is our little brother who was running away. We are taking him back," Salim said.

"No, wait. I smell something fishy."

"Then take this." Jackey took out his gun and pointed it at the man. "If you want to save your life, run, otherwise, I'll shoot you."

"No, let me go." The man ran towards the truck and got in. Salim and Jackey dragged Seby, and keeping him in between them, turned the bike and drove it at the top speed.

"Please let me go. You are like my elder brothers," Seby pleaded them as they drove the bike.

"Shut up you, devil. I had got up in the night and saw your bed empty. That made us to chase you," Jackey said.

"We believe in our business and don't trust in any relationship," Salim remarked.

"You wait and see what's in store for you as we take you back to our boss!" There was a threatening tone in Jackey's voice which made Seby shiver with fright.

When they came back to the house, Chakrapani was awake. Seeing the Don, Seby was almost frozen.

The boys told him about Seby's attempt to run away.

Chakrapani was fuming with anger. He clenched his fist and banged on the table. His face was as black as thundercloud. Seby was paralyzed with fear.

The Don flew at the kid, seized him by his throat, shook him hard and threw him to the wall. Then *grabbed* a cane and began to flog him mercilessly. The poor kid writhed in pain and cried aloud. The criminal kicked him and pushed him against the wall. Jackey and salim just enjoyed the cruelty.

"So you, a little devil, wanted to escape from us and report to the police to keep us behind the bar!"

The Don yelled. The man looked a real devil.

"I...eh... I only wanted to run away. I didn't want to report to the police," Seby *mustered* some courage and groaned.

"You said that you were sick and I showed some consideration, but you tried to fool me," the Don shouted at him as he continued *flogging* him. "Don't ever expect any more mercy from me."

The villain stopped his beating only when his hands began to ache.

"Both of you, boys, will get your special reward for the great work you have done," the Don told Jackey and Salim. Both the boys smiled. "As we have planned out, we are going to kidnap Iqbal's son, tomorrow. Go and get ready for the *'expedition'*."

"Yes, boss. We will succeed in our adventure, I'm sure," Jackey said with confidence.

The boys dragged the poor kid back to his bed and left him there to cry bitterly.

He was made to starve for one more day as part of the punishment. Chakrapani and his gang made sure that the boy would never try to escape again.

10

Super Kid busts a criminal conspiracy

The fateful day dawned.

SP Vikram was in his bungalow. He had two children, Jay and Vijay, who were also studying in Green Valley School, in the third and fifth classes. His wife was a software engineer. The children were ready to go to their school. Their driver used to drop them. The children waved their hands, said 'ta - ta' to their parents and sat in their Swift. SP Vikram and his wife too waved their hands.

The SP looked a bit upset. His wife, Savitri, immediately understood that something was disturbing him.

"What's the matter, dear? What's worrying you today?" she enquired with a lot of concern.

"It's about Chakrapani and his gang, of course. It has become my prestige issue. I've to give answer to my superior, as why the criminals have not yet been brought to book. The gang keeps on looting and kidnapping children from rich families. Let's do hope that they don't target our children."

"Oh, my God! Don't frighten me, dear. You are a brave and an honest police officer and have strong support of your police force. Then why to worry at all? I've trust in my husband's efficiency," though she *pacified* him, she too was tensed.

"Yes, I was only just sharing my apprehensions with my darling wife, not to scare you. I'm sorry, dear."

"It's okay, darling. You are going to bust the criminals today. Have faith in God and in your capability and everything is going to be fine."

"I do hope so. I was once successful in putting Chakrapani and his gang behind the bar, but you know, the influence of the corrupt politicians. Some of them, with stint in their character, got them released. Okay, now it's getting late, let me go."

The SP's Honda City took him to the police station and soon he became immersed in various law and order issues.

Chakrapani and his gang proceeded to Green valley school in the evening. By now the school was over and Riaz was taken by the driver in their BMW towards their mansion. The gang followed the car in a van. Then taking a short-cut road they overtook the BMW and blocked their way. To avoid a collision, the driver stopped the car.

"Hey, what's the matter? How dare you stop us?" The driver opened the window glass and shouted at them.

Riaz was reading a comic book and wondered why the driver stopped the car.

"Soon you will get the answer, you ......" Chakrapani lowered the window and answered after showering a number of abuses at him, "We are interested only in the kid. Hand over him to us and then we will spare you. If not, we won't mind sending a bullet to crack your brain!"

The driver was a well-built and a brave man. He told them boldly, "as long as I am alive, you are not going to take him away."

"Then, boys, come out and take the kid. Let me see how he is going to stop us."

Patel, Jaffar and Vicky Singh opened the door and rushed at the BMW, opened its door and dragged Riaz out. The boy started crying and tried to escape, but in vain. They took him into their van. Vicky Singh gave a severe blow on the driver's head and sped away. The driver fell unconscious.

At this time Jim and other kids had reached their home. Jim was drinking tea and there was a tickle in his brain. The whole episode was revealed to him as on a screen. Jim continued drinking tea, but his other self, Super Kid, appeared in front of SP Vikram. The SP was alone in his office, checking some files. When he closed the file and looked up, he was surprised to see a kid in a strange outfit standing in front of him.

"Hey, who are you? Who allowed you to come inside?" The SP asked him.

"Sir, I am known as Super Kid. You must have read about me in the newspaper, as how I had saved a child from drowning. I know that you are in search of the hideout of Chakrapani and his gang. I have just seen them kidnapping a child, named Riaz, who was going home when the school got over. They have hit the driver on his head. The poor fellow is bleeding and needs urgent hospitalization. The gang has just left the poor fellow near the Chinese restaurant near the fly-over and headed towards their *hide-out*, which is far inside a jungle. If you come with me taking your police force, you can catch them and save the child."

'Yes, I've read about you in the newspaper but I couldn't believe it. Any way, if what you are telling me is to be believed, there is no time to lose. Take us first to the car where the driver is lying and then we will chase the gang."

"Only you will be able to see me. Whenever you want to talk with me when others are around, you may use your mobile. They will think that you are talking on the phone."

"That's a good idea!"

The SP rang the calling bell and a police man appeared at the door.

"Call all the policemen, ask them to take the guns and be ready to chase a gang."

The SP carried his fully loaded service revolver and rushed out. They got into the police van and all the vehicles headed towards the spot where the driver was lying. Super Kid was sitting next to the SP but he was invisible to the police force.

As soon as they reached the car, some policemen were ordered to take the driver to a hospital, and others rushed to hunt for the criminals.

The gang had taken the jungle road. Super Kid made the wheels of their van punctured using his power. They could not go any further. To their horror, they soon heard the sound of the approaching police van and saw that there were many policemen along with SP Vikram.

"Come on; run with your full speed. None of us should be caught by them." Chakrapani gave orders and all of the gang took to their heels through their familiar track in the jungle. One of them picked up Riaz and ran at his full speed.

Now Super Kid thought, "let there be a heavy rain." At once the sky turned cloudy and it began to pour down. Soon there was a landslide. Water gushed forth from the hillside and flowed down into the hide – out of the gang. The gang was wonderstruck at the sudden phenomenon and couldn't run ahead at all. Some tried to climb over the rocks and swim down, but they slipped and fell down.

At once the SP ordered one of the policemen to snatch Riaz from the gang. Once it was done the police force *pounced* upon the gang like a tiger on its prey. Soon all of them were caught and taken to their van.

SP Vikram turned to Riaz and asked his name and the

school. He was surprised to learn that he was the son of his best friend, Iqbal sir. SP Vikram just patted on him affectionately and said, "I'm happy to learn that you are the son of my close friend, Iqbal sir. Now don't worry. You are safe with us. I am going to inform him that you are safe now."

Riaz was relieved now and felt quite comfortable.

The SP, keeping his mobile near to the ear, whispered to Super Kid, "Thank you, dear Super Kid, for your help. If you hadn't come for our assistance, we would not have succeeded to nab this *notorious* gang." The policemen thought that he was talking on his phone.

"I would rather give the credit to God, it's all His doing. All glory to Him alone," Super Kid whispered in SP Vikram's ears.

Riaz was crying all the way, but now he was full of astonishment at all the happenings and at his miraculous escape from the gang. He watched and enjoyed the chase by the police.

Super Kid, now appeared before Riaz and whispered in his ear, "Don't wonder, but thank God for your escape. May He protect you always! Don't tell anyone about me."

Riaz was excited to hear the words of Super Kid.

Saying this he just vanished from there.

At once he appeared inside the hide-out of the gang. Salim and Jacky were keeping a watch over Seby, who was just lying on his bed. Super Kid saw them and started thrashing the gang with his baton. Before they realized what was happening, they were under continuous shower of blows. Seby got up and wondered at the sudden turn of events.

"Seby, dear, you don't worry any longer. God has been gracious to you. I am known as Super Kid and have come to rescue you from here," Super Kid consoled him.

Seby thought that he was seeing a dream. Super Kid, using his power, made the gang to get into their vehicle and to drive to the police station. SP Vikram was informed about the gang and, he in turn, asked the local police to catch the gang. The Sub Inspector, with the help of a few policemen, caught the complete gang that day.

Seby was taken to his home by the police. To everyone's shock, they found the door of the house was locked.

When enquired, the neighbours said that the family had moved away and no one knew where they had gone. They further told them that their daughter was very sick and the parents had no money to treat her as they had to shell out all their earnings to the thugs as ransom for their son's life. Though the gang had promised to return Seby, they didn't keep their promise. The family had turned pauper and no one came to their help. In utter disappointment, without telling anyone, they went away to a remote place.

One of the neighboures whispered, "I think that as they had become very poor, the man must have gone to some faraway place to do labourer's work.

It's a prestige issue, you see, to work here among the familiar people."

Hearing the account given by the neighbours, Seby sat down in utter *despair*.

"I hoped that my bad days were over and that I could meet my parents and my dear sister. Where am I going to search for them, will I ever see them again?" Seby wept. Others tried to console him, but to no avail.

"God will be kind to you; He won't leave you in despair. Believe in God's providence and you will find your dear ones soon." Super Kid's words had magical powers which made Seby *optimistic*. The police took Seby to an *orphanage* and he began to spend his life there, hoping that one day he would be able to rejoin his family.

11

Seby's reunion with his family

A week passed. A shocking incident was taking place in the City hospital, quite far away. The hospital management had refused to admit a patient who was in a critical condition as the poor parents couldn't pay the deposit amount. Their plea and the miserable condition of the patient had no impact on them.

"We are running the hospital for profit and not for charity." The Director of the hospital, an arrogant man, told them *bluntly*. The condition of the patient was growing more and more critical. Her parents had lost all hope. The mother sat crying and looked helplessly at her daughter.

The girl's father went out, bought a big jar of kerosene, and managed to reach the terrace unnoticed by the security and the hospital staff. He locked the door leading to the terrace and began to pour kerosene all over the hospital building.

The security noticed him and shouted, "Hey, idiot, what are you up to? STOP!!"

Everyone got the smell of kerosene and there was great *panic* around. The security and the staff rushed to the terrace and began to bang at it.

"Go down, or I will set fire to the hospital immediately!" The man shouted from the terrace.

People gathered down in front of the hospital. Everyone was looking towards the man, with horror writ on their faces.

"Don't move. Don't call the police or the fire brigade. I am fully disappointed by the callous attitude of the hospital management. I am bent to teach them a lesson." The man screamed from the terrace.

"But the patients who are admitted in the hospital will suffer. Don't take any drastic step." One of the senior doctors shouted from the yard.

"I don't care. I want the Director of the hospital to kneel down there and ask my pardon. He must agree to treat my daughter without taking the deposit." The man spoke *resolutely*.

The Director now came out and shouted at the top of his voice, "You fool, do what you want. I am not going *to cow down* and do anything as you say. The police will come here soon and they will take care of you."

"If the police come here, or if any one of you dares to be extra smart to reach me here, I am going to drop this bomb which is in my bag!" He showed them a bag.

"I have lost all hopes. My daughter may die any time. I had a son, but I don't know his whereabouts. I have lost my children and my earnings. Why to live? I'll set fire to the hospital and set ablaze myself as well. This is my revenge!" The man held a lighter in his hand.

People understood that he was desperate and would do as he told them. The situation was becoming tense. There was panic, fear and uncertainty. The mother and daughter were in another part of the hospital and were unaware of the happening.

"If only Super Kid were to be here!" One of the children expressed hope.

At that time there was a tickle in Super Kid's mind. He visualized the whole situation. He just wished and instantly appeared at the sight. Everyone looked at him with awe and wonder.

"Uncle, don't take any drastic step. If you set fire to the hospital, you are going to kill your son too!" Super Kid shouted. "Look, who is with me here!"

The man looked down and saw his son Seby standing with Super Kid.

"Papa, I am back safely. Don't set fire. Please open the door and come down. I am longing to see you." Seby shouted with joy.

The man couldn't believe his eyes. "Am I dreaming? Is it my dearest son, Seby? " He asked with disbelief.

"Yes, Papa, I'm Seby. Come down soon."

"I will come down only, if these hospital *crooks* promise not to harm us and agree to treat my daughter."

"I assure you that no harm will come to any one of you." Super Kid told him.

Finally the man came down. Seby hugged him. The security examined his bag and to every one's delight and relief, there was no bomb but a toy instead! Seeing it everyone had a hearty laughter.

"You rascal, how dare you to fool us?" The director screamed. "We are not going to treat your daughter, let her die! Besides, the police will shut you down in the prison!"

Super Kid warned the hospital management not to take any action against the man but to treat the child properly that too without a deposit amount. He made the director to suffer from severe stomach pain. The man *reeled* in *agony*.

"How come this pain suddenly. Oh, I can't bear it any longer," the director writhed in agony.

"Until you agree to treat the girl without taking any fee, you are not going to be relieved," Super Kid said. "I am Super Kid with a noble mission, to help the needy and to punish the guilty."

He sent his baton at some of the doctors and it began to shower severe thrashing on them. The baton also thrashed some of the staff members who had refused to admit the girl. The hospital management had to give in and they agreed to treat the girl free of cost.

"You are running a hospital, not a *lucrative* business to *amass* money. Your *callous* attitude could have taken away a precious life. A doctor's duty is to try to save life and not to kill!" Super Kid told them sternly. "If you hand over the man to the police, you will have greater suffering and no doctor will be able to treat you!"

"No, please, no more suffering. I won't take any action against him," the director pleaded.

The man brought his wife and daughter. Great was the joy of the family in their reunion. Seby looked at his beloved sister, Celine, who was struggling for life. She opened her eyes and saw her loving brother. She smiled with relief. His mother had no words to express the joy she experienced in meeting her son again. Everyone thanked Super Kid profusely. He said humbly, "Thank God and not me. May his Holy name be glorified!" Saying this he disappeared suddenly.

"Now we have a Super Kid to help us in our needs and also to punish the guilty", an elderly man told another *bystander* and the latter agreed. Soon Celine began to recover. The family returned to their home and began to live happily there.

12

Super Kid Tackles Two Naughty Boys

Rahul and Roshan were the naughtiest children in the ninth standard. Both were the children of politicians and were the spoilt ones. Their fathers had no time to attend to them as they were busy with their election campaigns and other activities. Both Rahul and Roshan had beaten up another class mate. The reason was found out later on that the three were fond of a girl studying in the same class.

They were punished severely by their class teacher, Gaikwad sir, and the principal suspended them for a week. When both the boys were taken back in the school, they conspired to avenge for the punishment.

"Let us teach Gaikwad sir a lesson not to take any action against us again," Rahul told Roshan.

"I am also thinking in the same line. But how can we do it, dear?"

"Sir comes to the school on his bike, doesn't he? Let

us loosen the nuts of his bike and when he rides, he is sure to fall."

"Yes, what a fall it will be! There will be a fatal accident."

"Let him be in the hospital and we will be free from his scolding and punishment."

"Let's make sure that no one notices us, especially the Cheer up India club members. That boy, Jim, is very shrewd. I'm scared about him."

"I know. We must be extra cautious. If we are caught, the principal may give us Leaving Certificate."

"That will be drastic. We are sure to get good thrashing from our parents."

"We cannot bring spanner and screw driver to the school. We don't know when the Supervisor sir is going to arrange for a surprise checking of our school bags. He is very strict, isn't he?"

"I will get them from a friend's garage and let us hide them outside the gate. "

As planned out, the two friends managed to *sneak out* during the lunch break and decided to execute their villainous plan.

At that time, it tickled in Jim's brain and he realized his mission. He appeared as Super Kid and stood behind the boys as they had bent down to loosen the nuts. He had a baton in his hand and awarded severe thrashing to both the naughty ones! They writhed in pain and wondered who the figure was. They tried to catch hold of the baton from him, but got more beatings. The gate keeper rushed there and so also other children and the teachers.

The principal and the children recognized the unusual figure as Super Kid, who had appeared at the picnic spot and in the slum.

Super Kid told the principal, "Madam, please don't punish these boys again. I have given them good thrashing which they are bound to remember for the rest of their lives. They were trying to loosen the nuts of this bike to cause a fatal accident to Gaikwad sir. This is an unpardonable *juvenile* crime. Their parents have no time to look after them. These boys are in the bad company and getting spoiled day by day. If they don't reform themselves, I will be back with my baton again."

"Please don't beat us again. It's paining like anything," Rahul groaned.

"We will change our ways, for sure," added Roshan while crying.

"Then ask sir's pardon. Teachers must be treated with respect. The school is your second home and teachers are like your parents. They punish you to show you the right direction. Don't ever think of taking revenge." Super Kid wielded his baton menacingly.

"We are sorry for our unruly behaviour. We promise to change our ways for good."

The principal thanked Super Kid profusely and agreed to wait and watch whether the boys were going to change. She promised him that she wouldn't punish them that time.

"Please don't thank me. I am here to do God's work. Sometime God may choose to punish His children, when they go astray, His intention is to bring them in the right direction. Don't misunderstand God. He is love *incarnate* and kind. I chose to take up this step to give a warning to those who are very disruptive and mischievous. I am going to be tough with those who *turn deaf ears* to good advice. I won't spare the hard-hearted who try to inflict pain on others."

As they had focused their eyes on him, he just disappeared.

All were full of wonder as who the wonderful kid was and where he appeared from, at the nick of time.

"Who could be this Super Kid?" Ravi just wondered.

"Whoever he is, he's awesome!" Riaz said with great admiration.

"I can never forget his great help. If not for him I would have been dead," Vinay said. There were tears in his eyes.

"Why are you silent, Jim? What's your opinion about this Super Kid?" Marina asked innocently.

"I too wonder who he is. Whoever he may be, he's here on a noble mission." Jim said with a smile.

"Let's hope that one day he reveals himself." Jane expressed hope.

"We have only watched Superman, Batman, Shaktiman and Spiderman on the screen. But we are actually fortunate to meet a Super Kid!" Jerry was jubilant.

Super Kid's baton became a nightmare to those who were persistent trouble makers, the rowdy elements. At the same time there was great relief in the minds of the people. Soon all understood that Super Kid was *benevolent* to the good ones whereas a *terror* to the *rowdies*.

13

An Ideal Principal

The principal, Mrs. Susan, was a woman of great ideas and she loved the school children as her own. She used to spend a lot of time in meeting them personally in her office, especially the problematic ones, in order to learn about their problems, aspirations, and talents. She had undergone training in clinical psychology which helped her to give counseling to the needy children. She knew all the children by their names and used to visit their homes to keep rapport with their parents as well.

She was a mother to the children, a sister to the colleagues and a friend to the parents. She asked the teachers too, to be parents to the children, loving caring, guiding and encouraging. The school was actually a 'home away from home,' and learning there was fun.

She had received several awards, but she considered the children's progress and success as the real award which motivated her to do still better.

Iqbal sir, a great *humanitarian*, had given her full

freedom to run the school, with the least interference from the management.

She couldn't do much work in her previous school due to the interference of the management even in the smallest matters. She had found it difficult to work as a 'puppet principal' and resigned from the post. The principal, through her counseling, came to know many bitter truths. There were children from broken families, who were neglected because of fight between their parents. She came across children who were abused by others even by their own near ones. There were even children who had tried to commit suicide because of neglect and child abuses. One child had taken the extreme step of ending his life just after the SSC exams, because of the over expectation of the parents and the child's failure to meet the same.

After counseling a number of children, the principal called a meeting of the general body of PTA (Parent –Teachers Association) in which she voiced her observation and findings in very strong terms. Citing the example of the tragic death of the SSC student, the principal warned the parents to allow their children to live their lives and not to enforce their ambition on their children. If not, it could lead to painful and bitter experiences. The parents must try to understand their children, their likings and aspirations. She insisted that parents and teachers should work in *tandem* while developing children for a bright and successful future.

To help the children, she used to conduct awareness sessions, separately for girls and boys. Often resource persons were invited to manage the sessions.

In order to develop creativity in the children, one day she asked the children to prepare any creative work such as models or machines and she promised them that their work would be displayed in an exhibition. She also declared that the best creative works would be given attractive prizes.

Jim had made a small machine which was named, 'Handy Friend.' He made it with the help of old and dumped materials such as motor and speaker from a *discarded* tape recorder, tin sheets etc. He used his computer knowledge to do programming for the machine. The machine could pick up wrappers, papers, and other waste materials. It also could count answer papers, question papers and the speaker would announce the number of the count. It could work on battery or electricity.

'Handy Friend' was the attraction of the exhibition and it won the coveted first prize for being the best creative work. A function was held to give away prizes and Iqbal sir did the honour. Jim received ten thousand rupees cash prize, certificate and a memento. Many other children also received prizes for their creative contributions. Newspapers published the details of the exhibition with photographs.

Victor and Stella were the proud 'parents' to witness the success of their 'son'. Jane was excited by her brother's achievement. Victor and Stella gave full freedom to Jim to use the prize money. But Jim expressed his desire to contribute it to the Cheer up India club and they readily supported and encouraged his interest in humanitarian activities.

Mrs. Susan felt quite happy as the exhibition was

a grand success. Next she had to concentrate on the school inspection, which was scheduled after two days. She had to make sure that all the documents were up to date.

It was a Saturday and hence a holiday, yet she was alone in the office for a longer time to check the office files and was not even aware how the time passed. The peon, Jagtap, was on duty near her office and as it was getting late, he began to feel uneasy and restless. He knocked at her door and got inside.

"Madam, it's already 6 p.m.," Jagtap reminded her gently.

"Really? I was not aware of the time as I had some urgent work to be completed. Thank you, Jagtap, for reminding me about the time. Okay, I will shut down my computer and then you may lock the office."

She saved the files and shut down the computer.

She carried a few files with her in order to check them at home. She started her car and drove towards her residence. The sun was already set and street lights were on. She was lost in thought about the inspection. The road was almost vacant. She hadn't noticed a car following her. Suddenly it came from behind at full speed, overtook her Swift and stopped in its front, blocking her way.

Mrs. Susan applied brake and brought her car to a sudden stop. Two masked men came out of the car and rushed to her car. She had kept her windows down. One of the men pointed a gun at her and gestured her to step down from her car.

She was stunned. Horror was writ on her face. She looked around for help, but the street was empty. She kept on praying in her mind, "Merciful Lord, come to my help."

She tried to raise an alarm but one of the men screamed, "Don't act over smart madam, but come with us quietly. Otherwise we'll have to use force."

"What do you want? Leave me alone."

"Have patience," the other man said. "We will tell you everything once you get into our car"

Mrs. Susan had to follow their instruction. She knew that any resistance would lead to more troubles. As soon as they reached the car one of them pushed her to the seat. Then they sat on either side of her. She noticed that there was another man on the driver seat who had not worn mask.

"Who are you? Where are you taking me to?" She gathered some courage and enquired. "I haven't hurt anyone."

"Keep your mouth shut, madam. Let's go. Virendra, drive fast." One of the men asked the driver.

"You have many questions to ask us, we know. No more suspense. You say that you haven't hurt anybody, but I was hurt and disturbed because of you and was waiting to take revenge on you," the man paused.

"Now look at me and check whether you recognize me." He removed his mask and so did the other.

"You, VEERU DADA!!" She exclaimed.

"Good, so you haven't forgotten me." Veeru Dada grinned. "The other two are Vittal and Virendra."

"I had come to you to seek admission for my friend's child. In spite of my several requests, you bluntly refused to listen to me."

"Many students apply for admission in our school. We conduct tests every time and then select the deserving children only on the basis of merit. We neither take donations nor entertain recommendations. Your friend's child had scored the lowest marks, I still remember."

"You can't say 'no' to Veeru Dada, the dreaded Don," Virendra replied while driving the car.

The biggest blunder you made - you treated our boss like any other common visitor," Vittal said.

"Besides, we came to know that you and your friend were criminals, wanted by the police," Mrs. Susan added. "We never take children from such families which will *tarnish* the prestige of our school. Mr. Iqbal, the owner of our school, is very particular about it."

At the very moment Super Kid got a tickling and at once he reached the spot. He sat invisible next to the driver and listened to their conversation.

"You and your prestige! BAH!! I had approached Iqbal also for obtaining admission. But he did not even treat me with respect. I wanted to take revenge on him. Only because of luck he escaped from a car accident that I had created!"

"Oh, I see. Then it was you, VEERU DADA, who had

tried to kill Iqbal sir!" Super Kid told to himself. Super Kid recalled the incident vividly in his mind - someone sitting in a truck trying to create an accident by hitting at a car and pushing it down into a valley….. He also remembered how he made a police siren which made the gangster to drive away.

Super kid now made himself visible to Mrs. Susan and whispered in her ears, "Don't worry, I'm here to help you."

She was relieved greatly and thanked God for listening to her prayer.

"You wicked people can't do any harm to me because God is with me for my protection. He listens to our prayers and sends some good souls to save us," Mrs. Susan told them boldly.

"Let me see which 'good soul' comes to protect you," so saying Veeru Dada raised his right hand to slap her. At once his hand started shaking violently.

"What's happening? I….I can't stop my hand from shivering. It's paining severely. You idiot, Vittal, hold my hand," Veeru Dada screamed.

Vittal asked madam to take the window seat and after sitting next to his boss held his hand tightly but Vittal's hand also began shaking. Virendra pressed the brake and their car came to a sudden stop with a screeching sound. He too held the hands and tried to stop shaking, but in vain. All their hands were shaking violently and they felt severe and unbearable pain. They cried like babies.

Now Super Kid became visible to them. They were shocked.

"YOU, damn Super Kid again! Please stop this torture, I can't bear it any longer," Veeru Dada cried.

"Your hands will stop shaking only when you ask pardon from madam."

"We are sorry, madam," all the three screamed.

The hands stopped shaking and the trio felt relieved.

At once, Veeru Dada took out his gun, aimed at Super Kid and screamed, "FREEZE!"

"You are a criminal to the core, who is not prepared to change at all. But what are you holding?" Super Kid asked him.

Veeru Dada, the gang leader, glanced at his gun and to his great shock realized that he was holding a scorpion. Instantly he threw the creature away through the window.

"Now turn your car reverse and drive back where madam's car is parked."

"Virendra, do what this magician has told you," the Don said. "But where is my gun?"

"Forget your gun!" Super Kid said.

Virendra drove the car back towards madam's Swift. While going back the Don winked at Vittal and showed a gesture. Vittal understood the message and tried to open the door in order to push madam out of the running car.

Instantly they felt *excruciating* pain in their stomach. They pressed their belly with their hands and screamed.

"Ah! It's paining like anything. Please STOP!!" The Don yelled. Vittal also cried.

"Virendra, continue driving. If you try to do any mischief, you will also suffer stomach ache," Super Kid said.

"NO, please. I will follow whatever you say," Virendra said in a pleading tone.

Madam watched the happening and wondered at the great power that Super Kid had possessed.

Finally they could see madam's parked car and Virendra stopped their car.

"Madam, you may get into your car and drive home without any more trouble from these criminals." Super Kid said. "I will take care of them."

"Thank you, Super Kid, for your help."

"Don't thank me, be grateful to God, I'm only his humble messenger."

While Mrs. Susan was driving her car, Super Kid asked the gang to go from there and warned them sternly, "If ever you think of troubling madam, my baton will do the action. Remember – evil people can never enjoy real peace."

"We promise never to trouble her hereafter," the Don promised. They had to listen to Super Kid and went away, quite disappointed.

14

Escape of Chakrapani and his gang

Chakrapani and his gang were locked together in the same cell in the jail.

"We have never stayed so long in any jail. It's high time to escape from this *nasty* place. But, how…? Come on guys, think about some super plans." Chakrapani racked his brain for an idea and told his gang.

"The only way is bribing one of the guards, I feel," Jackey suggested.

"There are always some corrupt policemen who would fall prey to our *trap*." Salim backed Jackey.

"Just call that guard, let us try with him." Pointing to a guard, Chakrapani told Jackey.

Jackey called the policeman on guard, "My boss wants to talk to you. Come inside."

"Shut up, you idiot. I don't know any boss." The policeman spoke very rudely. He was enjoying a nap and having disturbed, he got quite irritated.

"We will be out of this place any time. No jail can keep us locked for a long time. If you cooperate with us we will reward you handsomely. If not, you and your family won't live in peace," said Salim with a threatening tone.

The guard became silent and thought for some time. He was worried about the security of his family. Besides, he was very greedy.

"How can I help you?"

"Come in. Our boss will tell you."

The guard had the key; using it he opened the door and went inside. Chakrapani smiled and asked the guard, "By the by, what's your name?"

"Sharma. What do you want me to do for you?"

"You can help us, if you are willing, and your reward will be great, unexpected, indeed!"

"Your offer is quite thrilling. Hope you will not change your promise after you get your work done."

"Don't you trust us? We are criminals but once we promise, believe it's done."

"Okay. Now tell me, how can I serve you?"

"The first thing is - I want a mobile phone to contact somebody outside. When the food is brought, hide it in the plate and get it for me. Next I need guns. Get at least five of them. "

"I can get the mobile, but guns.......it's very risky."

"Without pain, there is no gain!" Chakrapani looked at his gang and smiled. They admired his wisdom.

"Vow boss, you are a *genius*!" Jackey praised him but wondered what he had meant!

"Get *chloroform* as well," Salim added.

"I have a friend outside, who will get the guns and chloroform for you. You only have to get them for us here." Chakrapani continued.

As planned, Sharma got the mobile phone and chloroform the next day. Chakrapani managed to make the urgent calls without any other guard's notice and got the required guns.

Sharma carried the food inside the cell and told Chakrapani, "You make me unconscious using the chloroform. Then take the key from me, open the cell and escape. But when can I get my reward?"

"Don't worry man. After our escape, I will call you. Come to our hideout in the jungle and I will reward you *aptly* for all your support." Chakrapani patted Sharma's back.

Chakrapani and his gang waited for the opportune time for their escape. As suggested by Sharma, they made him unconscious using chloroform, dragged him inside the cell, came out and locked the prison from outside. Then they stealthily moved on the corridor. A guard noticed them and was about to make an alarm.

Jackey acted immediately and at the gun point, bound him and made him unconscious using chloroform.

Salim, brought all the guards unconscious in the same way and thus finally the gang managed to escape successfully. Chakrapani's aid was waiting outside with an Omni van and all sped up to safety.

The gang had made their hideout in a new place, deep inside a dense forest. Their van came to a halt near a forest. That was the dead end of the road. But surprisingly the driver banged the van against the creepers that had blocked the way, and a road was seen in front of them.

The van stopped after running a few meters. The gang jumped out of the van and ran to the entrance and placed back the 'gate' made with the help of artificial creepers. Now the forest looked the same as before. No one could make out that a road ran through the forest. Both sides were covered with thick thorny bushes, which prevented anyone from coming inside that part of the forest. There were gangs with *lethal* weapons who kept watch twenty four hours at different spots in the forest.

All around the border of the forest, nails were planted to prevent any vehicle from coming inside. A guard, after making sure that the vehicle belonged to Chakrapani, put his fingers on a device and a platform with nails went down and up came a metal bridge. The van passed through the bridge. The moment the van passed the bridge, the platform with nails came up.

The van ran for half an hour and then it stopped near a bungalow, deep inside the jungle. Chakrapani and the gang were jubilant about their adventurous escape and began to plan further villainous activities.

15

Chakrapani's hide-out in the jungle

The next morning, Chakrapani asked Salim to bring Sharma, the guard, who had helped the gang to escape from the jail. Salim bought him on his bike and as they reached somewhere near the forest, he blindfolded the guard.

"Hey, what are you doing man? You can trust me. I won't betray you." Sharma told Salim a bit disturbed by the lack of trust Salim had put on him.

"It's part of our way of operation. We don't take risks, you see." Salim told firmly.

"How far is your place?" Sharma was becoming disturbed.

"No more questions. Wait and see."

Thereafter Sharma didn't dare to ask anything more. He now understood that it was wise to remain quiet and watch what was going to happen. He was becoming *apprehensive* as whether helping a *dreaded* gang to escape was right or not.

After riding for half an hour, they reached the gang's hideout. Now Salim alighted and led Sharma inside the bungalow. He removed his blindfolding. Sharma looked around and surprised to find himself in a well - furnished hall, that too surrounded by forest. Sharma was taken to a big hall.

He saw Chakrapani sitting on a royal chair. His guards and the gang were also in the hall.

"Welcome Sharma to our humble cottage," Chakrapani said and the gang laughed.

"You are joking. This is not less than a palace!"

"Yes, Chakrapani and his gang are destined to live in a palace and not in your filthy stinking damn jail!" Again the gang had a hearty laugh.

"I am happy, rather excited to be here. I really thank you for remembering me and calling me here as promised by you."

"So you want the reward for helping us, don't you?"

"I am growing very impatient. I know my reward will be great. You are enjoying freedom once again because of my help."

"Okay, now take your reward!" Chakrapani took out a pistol suddenly and pointed it at Sharma.

Sharma shivered and his face turned pale.

"If anyone asks for a reward, Chakrapani is ready for him. This is called 'Chakrapani style'!"

There was a roar of laughter in the hall.

"How dare you, a mere rat, to demand a reward from this mighty lion?"

"But ....you had promised me," Sharma stammered.

"Shut up you swine, no one dares to talk to our boss thus." Salim shouted and slapped Sharma.

"You were a fool to trust us, Chakrapani doesn't keep promises. He gets rid of evidence," Chakrapani grinned.

Looking at the Don, he knew that anytime, this cruel criminal may send a bullet to get rid of him. He shuddered at the thought. He realized with regret that he had made the biggest blunder.

"Lock him up in a cell. Let him experience what is life in a jail." Chakrapani put his pistol away. "Take his mobile away."

Sharma heaved a sigh. "For the time being, my life is spared!" He said to himself.

Salim pushed him into a dirty room. Behind him the iron door was closed with a creaking sound.

Sharma sat down desperate and full of remorse for his criminal action. He thought about his family and wondered whether he would be able to escape from there any time.

"What a grave crime I have committed, helping a dreaded gang to escape." Sharma said to himself. "I was supposed to prevent the criminals from escaping but I too have become a criminal now. How can I call myself a policeman?"

Meanwhile the family of Sharma was in utter distress. Sharma's wife and the only son, Ravi, were worried as Sharma was found missing. Both went to the jail superintend, Wilson.

"What's the matter, Mrs. Sharma, both of you look worried," Wilson asked them.

"My husband is missing. Yesterday, as usual, he went out for the duty. But he didn't return at the usual time. Then I called up here and came to know that he hadn't come for duty at all."

"I see. Didn't you call him on his phone?"

"I tried several times but his mobile was switched off. We doubt whether something has happened to him."

"Take courage. I will make arrangements to enquire about him. You must have already heard that a gang escaped from the jail. Sharma was a guard to watch them but his disappearance has disturbed us as well. Any way, it is too early to comment on the matter. Which class are you studying in, son?" Wilson enquired Ravi.

"I am now in seventh standard. Sir, please find out my dad."

"Don't worry, son. Your dad will be back soon."

The firmness in Wilson's voice *consoled* them and they left the office with some relief.

Ravi went to the school next day. He was very silent that day and sat quite upset and perturbed. During the recess, his friends gathered around him to enquire what made him disturbed.

"What's the matter Ravi, you look very worried," Jerry asked Ravi.

"My dad has not returned from his duty. Actually he neither attended his duty during the day nor returned home in the evening. We are worried about him."

"He must have gone out for his duty. Wait for some more days. After all, he is a policeman." Marina told him.

"Our worry is why his mobile is switched off and how come we are not able to contact him."

"Have you reported to the Jail Superintend?" Riaz enquired.

"Of course, my mom and I went to him yesterday and the officer has assured that he will take care of the matter. But until dad returns, we have no peace."

"I wonder where Super Kid is. If he had known about uncle's missing, he would have surely found out him," Vinay said. He recalled the sudden appearance of Super Kid at the pond and how he had saved him from the swamp.

Other friends too tried to console him.

Meanwhile the jail Superintend, Wilson, had informed SP Vikram about the escape of Chakrapani and his gang and about the disappearance of Sharma.

Veeru Dada's attempts to be a Don

Veeru Dada's greatest ambition was to become a Don more powerful than Chakrapani. He had a gang who would do anything for him. He wanted money to pursue his ambitious and devilish plan.

One day, he called his gang and had a detailed discussion as how to raise a large 'fund'.

"Haven't you heard about Chakrapani? He is a king of the underworld without a crown. I want to become greater than him, in fact, he should be afraid of me. The first thing is, we must have a lot of money. Money is power. Money can buy anything, including respect and fame. If we have a lot of wealth, I would have lived like a king and you would have been my ministers. Tell me how can we become richer?" He asked his gang.

"I feel that sale of drug is a flourishing business," suggested, Vittal, one of the gangsters.

"To me smuggling also can bring in a lot of money," opined Virendra.

"I was also thinking about both the ways. Let us start with drug sale. We have a good collection of drugs. I want our gang to start selling drugs using school children."

"But why using school children, boss?" Vittal enquired.

"That's because the police may not suspect them. Be careful about that damn Super Kid. I have not forgotten the taste of his baton, still now."

"Engaging children in our business is a good idea, boss. You are a genius." Vittal was full of admiration for Veeru Dada and the latter enjoyed such compliments.

Next day, the gang stood near the Green Valley School. Soon they saw Rahul and Roshan coming to the school. They were, as usual, shouting and playing some pranks as they moved to the school. Virendra pointed at them and told Vittal: "Look at them. I think they will help us to sell drugs here."

"I too share your view. They may be the trouble makers in the school. We can train them to be criminals."

"We shall train them and they will drag other children into the business. We can thus spread our web. We shall start here and then we can extend to other schools."

"Yes, we should also be rich like Chakrapani."

Virendra called Rahul and Roshan as they approached near.

"Come on boys, in which class are you studying?" Vittal put his hands on their shoulders and asked in a friendly manner.

"Who are you, uncle? "Why do you want to know about us?" Rahul asked angrily.

"We are your well wishers. Don't you like earning some pocket money while studying?" Vittal spoke in a diplomatic manner.

"Earning pocket money? What have we to do?" enquired Roshan getting interested.

"You can earn not just pocket money, much, I would say very much more than what you can just imagine, if only you follow our instructions." Virendra knew that they had found the most suitable boys to do their business and he winked at Vittal.

"We wanted to buy the latest mobile phone. If you can offer us sufficient money to turn our dream into reality, we can think about doing the work for you. We are students of class IX. Now tell us what we have to do. At the same time, we don't want to get into trouble," Rahul was very clear.

"If you follow our instructions carefully and do the work for us, you will earn much more than what you can even dream! Not only mobile, but you can even buy motor bike, lap top, watch any number of movies and have dinner parties in star hotels….." Vittal said while watching the expression on the faces of the boys and winked at Virendra.

"Let us move behind that shop. We don't want other children to hear us." Vittal told them in a whisper.

All moved behind a shop that had its shutters down. Now Vittal continued making sure that nobody could hear them and then told them: "You have to sell this 'booster medicine' to your companions in your school. Collect the amount you receive from them and give us at the end of the day. We shall pay you monthly. Your earning will depend upon the number of packets you sell every day."

"What's the guarantee that you will pay us after we sell the products?" Rahul was a bit *skeptical*.

"Okay, take one thousand each as your advance, as a token money!" Virendra took out the amount and gave one thousand each to both of them. They were really surprised.

"Okay, so you mean business. Now tell us what you mean by this '*booster* medicine'.

"It's booster powder. Both of you take some sample. You will feel very strong, energetic and happy. Then you can memorize your lessons better, faster. You will be the heroes in your school. In short, you can enjoy your life!" Vittal said and smiled encouragingly.

"That will be great," Rahul imagined riding a super bike and coming to the school. Roshan also dreamed going for parties with his friends, wearing expensive suit and driving his own luxury car!

Virendra took some powder and gave it to each of them.

"Do you know what's this powder called?"

"I have seen it in the films. It is drugs, I suppose." Rahul said.

"You are right. You take it and experience the fun for yourself."

At the very moment, Super Kid got a tickling. He saw the happening and reached the spot instantly. He noticed that the kids were about to take the dangerous drug. He remained invisible and immediately blew on their hands and the powder was blown away.

"I wonder where such a damn wind comes suddenly from nowhere!" Virendra screamed furiously. He took out another pinch and told Rahul: "Open your mouth and I will drop the powder on your tongue."

As Virendra was about to drop the powder, suddenly he got a violent jerk, and the powder was blown away again. He suffered *severe* pain on his hand.

"What the hell is going on? Ah! My hand is paining as if someone is hitting on it with a sharp knife. But what happened suddenly? I fail to understand."

"Don't worry, I will give them the drug," Vittal came forward and took another pinch and advanced towards the boys. As he approached them, Super Kid gave him a mighty kick from behind. Vittal fell on his face and the powder got scattered in the air. As he struggled to his feet, blood oozed out from his forehead.

"Something *weird* is happening here; I suspect whether this place is *enchanted!*" Virendra cried.

"I doubt whether our enemy, that Super Kid, may be somewhere here!" Vittal wiped the blood and told his companion. Virendra shuddered hearing it. Both had heard from Veeru Dada how Super Kid had thrashed him with his baton when he and his gang had made fun of the school children during the Cheer up India campaign.

Rahul and Roshan were shocked and shivered hearing Super Kid's name. They remembered the severe beating they got when they had played pranks on Gaikwad sir.

"If he is here, he is surely somewhere very near to us. Let us take a stick and beat in the air, he may get hurt," Virendra suggested. He looked around and noticed a pipe lying nearby. He picked it up and began to beat in the air, like a mad man. Suddenly he realized that the pipe was turning extremely hot and it almost burnt his palms. He instantly dropped it down with a scream.

Vittal saw a piece of a plank, raised it and waved it around, but suddenly he was frozen and stood like a statue.

"Vittal, my dear friend, what happened? Why don't you move?" Virendra tried to shake him and suddenly he too turned a statue. They were still holding the packets of drugs in their out stretched hands.

Watching their plight, Rahul and Roshan were shocked and tried to run away. At once Super Kid's baton appeared in the air and gave a few beating to both the boys. They began to cry. After some time Super Kid appeared in front of them. Their faces turned pale as if they saw a ghost in front of them suddenly.

"I had warned you to give up your pranks, but you were about to turn criminals by selling drugs even to your own companions in the school." Super Kid gave them one more thrashing each and the boys writhed in pain. They yelled bitterly.

"Do you know the gravity and seriousness of what you were about to commit?" Super Kid asked them furiously. "Consuming and selling drugs is one of the worst crimes. Addiction to drugs has destroyed many lives. You wanted to earn easy money and enjoy life. But remember money collected by unfair and evil ways won't last. You are students and your duty is to study and not to turn criminals."

"We are extremely sorry, we will stop all our pranks," Rahul cried.

"You will have to confess your crime to your principal madam. I will be meeting her personally. Now you may go to your school, to avoid being late."

Rahul and Roshan wiped their tears and rushed to the school. Children had started standing for the assembly. They kept their bags in the class room and hurried to join their classmates.

Super Kid had already informed SP Vikram about Veeru Dada's attempt to sell drugs to school children using his gangsters, Virendra and Vittal. SP Vikram rushed there with a few policemen from Anti-Narcotics Cell and *nabbed* them red handed, carrying drugs. As soon as the police came there, Super Kid released the criminals from being frozen.

After the assembly, Rahul and Roshan went to the principal, Mrs. Susan, and told her about the happening of that morning. "YOU,....you were going to join the criminals to sell drugs to my children!" She screamed and banged on the desk. "I am going to *rusticate* both of you."

"Madam, we are extremely sorry for our behavior. Hereafter we will be good children," Rahul *pleaded*.

"We promise never to misbehave hereafter. Those criminals were misleading us. If you rusticate us, we will be beaten severely by our parents." Roshan was in tears.

"But how come, they chose only you out of other childen? The criminals understood from your behaviour that you have a tendency to do mischief. I had not forgotten what you were about to do to Gaikwad sir."

"After you had given us the warning we have not disturbed Gaikwad sir anymore," Rahul defended.

"That's okay, but are you aware what would have been the *repercussion* of your actions, if Super Kid hadn't appeared at the *nick of time*? You would have turned criminals selling drugs and destroying the lives of my children here. I can't even imagine my children getting spoiled thus. Now, both of you go back to your class. Right now I am busy and very much disturbed. I will call you back later on." The principal leaned back on her chair, utterly perturbed, closed her eyes and tried to keep herself calm.

Suddenly there was a knock at the door and as she opened her eyes she couldn't believe her eyes. Super Kid stood in front of her! He wore a mask which hid his identity, but lips were open and she could see the smile on his face. She was excited, and greatly pleased to see him and felt great relief.

Super Kid narrated the incident. Mrs. Susan promised him that she would take all necessary steps to curb any more such criminal activities in the school. She also told him that she was planning to arrange a special talk by SP Vikram to create awareness among the children about drug abuse. After an assurance from her, he appeared in front of SP Vikram.

SP Vikram was in his office. Super Kid told him about the principal's plan to have an awareness session and suggested him to arrange some policemen to keep a regular watch around educational institutes so that the criminals could be prevented or nabbed from their undesirable activities, like selling of drugs, eve teasing, fighting and other criminal activities.

Veeru Dada was quite *crestfallen* after the arrest of two of his strong *henchmen* – Virendra and Vittal. He sat upset for some time and then thought about a plan to *compensate* for the loss.

17

A bank robbery

The arrest of Virendra and Vittal was like a thunderbolt for Veeru Dada. He had lost drugs worth crores. Besides, two of his trusted men, Virendra and Vittal, were in the jail. He was furious and utterly desperate. He called his gang and discussed with them about their future plans.

"Now our loss is tremendous, and its recovery is next to impossible," Veeru Dada told his gang. "I am all the more disturbed about, Super Kid, who is our bitterest enemy number one and the second is SP Vikram. Unless and until they are 'dispatched' from the earth, we can't do our business and live in peace."

"But it's not at all an easy task!" Mangal, a dreaded criminal, expressed his apprehension.

"You fool; I know that better than you do. I want suggestions and ideas and not such comments!" Veeru Dada screamed. Mangal felt insulted, but he had to bear it.

"I am planning to attack Chakrapani and loot his

wealth. I feel that's the best idea to make up for our loss," the Don looked around for a positive response and his gang readily agreed. Veeru Dada and Chakrapani had some heated arguments earlier. Chakrapani had looted some of Veeru's booty in the past before he had become a dreaded Don.

Down his memory lane Veeru recalled the happenings on that most unfortunate day. One day Veeru and his gang prepared a detailed plan to loot a petrol pump in an *isolated* place. They planned to do the operation late in the night. That particular petrol pump was kept open till twelve in the night.

The time was then 11.45 and the road was almost vacant except for some youngsters going for their night shift work. Virendra and Vicky, after making sure that nobody was around, went to the petrol pump on a bike. That time only three people were in the petrol pump, one among them was inside the camp, counting the day's collection. Other two were engaged in serving petrol to the customers.

Virendra was riding his bike and Vicky was the *pillion* rider. As the duo reached the petrol pump, they alighted. Virendra asked the man at the pump to fill rupees three hundred worth petrol. As he began to drop petrol, Virendra applied some chloroform on his kerchief and suddenly covered the man's face with it. The man collapsed there, without making any noise. The other man, with his back turned to them, was counting the day's collection. Virendra rushed to him, made him also to smell the chloroform and he too fell backwards, unconscious. The man in the cabin was not aware of the happening outside.

With the same kerchief Virendra and Vicky, next went to the cabin and opened its door slowly. As the man turned back to see as who had entered the room, Virendra acted swiftly with the chloroform and the poor chap also fell unconscious. The man had counted the amount and had arranged it in bundles, which made it easy for the gang to grab it and run away to safety.

While the duo was running away with the loot, Chakrapani and Jackey pounced upon them on the way. Both had worn masks to hide their identity. Chakrapani meanwhile had asked Salim to keep a watch over the duo. Salim had watched the operation carried out by Virendra and Vicky by hiding behind the petrol pump and promptly reported it to his boss. After some struggle, Chakrapani and Jackey managed to overpower the duo. While the struggle was going on, Vicky succeeded in pulling their masks and noticed the faces behind. Leaving the masks, both the criminals, Chakrapani and Jackey, fled with the loot. It was a severe blow to Veeru Dada and he always looked forward for a chance to avenge the loss and the humiliation.

The robbery had come to limelight only in the morning when someone had come for filling petrol and the guy rang up to the nearby police station.

As Veeru recalled the incident he became half mad with rage. He thought about a plan to compensate for the loss and to take revenge on Chakrapani. He called

Mangal, one of his gang members, a sturdy fellow, and told him, "You come with me. We are going for an operation!"

"In which hospital, boss? Are you not well?" Mangal asked quite innocently.

"Idiot! You know only the operation done in the hospital. Our operation is different. Don't we want to avenge Chakrapani for looting us in the past? Now time is ripe to teach him a lesson. We are going to kidnap one of his loyal men to know Chakrapani's future plans. How's my idea?"

"The idea is super, boss. I'm with you."

"Yes, that's the spirit. If we can catch hold of Jackey, it will be great."

"Jackey goes to gym every morning. That is the right time because the roads are not at all crowded then."

"That's right. We will have the operation tomorrow early morning."

Next day, the duo waited near the gym. Then they saw Jackey coming on his bike.

Veeru Dada and Mangal, stopped his bike at gunpoint and asked him to go along with them. Both had covered themselves to conceal their identity. Jackey resisted, but, in vain. Mangal tied his hands behind, fixed a bandage on his mouth, blindfolded him, pushed him into their car and went to their hide-out.

As soon as they reached their destination, Mangal removed the blindfold and pulled out the bandage.

"Hey, who are you? You don't know who I am; otherwise you would not have dared to do this *feat*!" Jackey yelled.

"You want to know who we are, no problem. Have a look at us," Veeru Dada removed his mask as he said it. "We know each other very well, I suppose, Jackey, the right hand of Chakrapani!"

"It's you, Veeru Dada! My boss, Chakrapani, will not spare you once he comes to know it," Jackey screamed.

"Don't worry, Jackey, we are yet to decide whether we should spare you or not!"

"Untie me, you *coward*, and I will show you who I am."

"You are under our custody, and we can do anything to you now, there is none around here to save you."

"You are underestimating the power of my boss, the dreaded Don!"

"Shut up! Dreaded Don, Chakrapani! BAH! I am not scared of that *buffoon*! Mark it; I too am another dreaded Don, Veeru Dada the great!!"

"What do you want from me, speak up."

"Have patience! Don't dare to order me! We will answer all your questions soon. Now listen carefully. I want you to join hands with us. Leave your boss."

"It's impossible!"

"I will make it possible! If you don't listen to us, you won't live to see the next morning!"

"I am not scared. I will fight till my last breath."

"Don't be foolish. First listen to our plan, which is good for your future. Okay, you don't have to leave your boss. Remain in your group and help us out. Your reward will be great."

"You mean, spy work for you! I don't want to *betray* my boss!"

"We all are criminals, and no way out of it. Be practical and you will benefit if you follow our plan. All of us want money. What you have to do is a very simple work, just report to us about your plans, about your wealth etc. We want a person there who is loyal to us, and we will be rewarding you *handsomely* for the same. We shall share our earnings with you. You can remain with your boss and at the same time, be our men."

"I have to think about it."

"No way, Jackey, we allow you no time to think. Your only option is to agree. Suppose you don't agree with our proposal, you know what's going to happen to you? We WILL KILL you. We can't take risks, you see."

"I understand"

"So you have no choice, only just agree with our proposal, and you will become rich. Otherwise you will not be able to see the tomorrow! So then, Jackey, what do you want, to live and earn or have a miserable death?"

"I have no choice then, but to accept your proposal."

"Yes, Jackey, just agree with us and let us be friends."

"Okay then, I will be your man working for you from the side of my boss, Chakrapani."

"Take fifty thousand as a token money; spend it *lavishly* for your enjoyment. Now tell us what is your next plan, looting bank or shops, tell us about the operation *frankly* and in detail. If what you tell us is truth, we shall reward you again in lakhs!"

"Next we are planning to loot the 'Customer- friend cooperative bank', near the Central store."

Jackey then narrated the plan of their operation.

"We are happy that you have agreed to cooperate with us. But we can't trust all that you said, because we don't know each other well. You may act smart. So you take this hidden camera and handle it carefully. If your boss comes to know about it, he will definitely kill you. Using this camera, we can see what's going on there and listen to your conversations."

"Now I have no other way, but to listen to you. I am caught badly!"

"Don't say, caught. You are going to be a wise one. I would say you are a lucky, wise and practical guy!"

After taking the amount, Jackey left for Chakrapani's hideout. He followed Veeru Dada's instructions faithfully.

A well-knit plan was prepared for looting the 'Customer friendly cooperative bank' next week. The gang of Chakrapani entered the bank during the lunch break at gun point. Only a few of the staff members were in the bank at that time, as others were having their meals together in a closed cabin. One of the members of the gang tied the security guard and covered his mouth with a bandage. Then the gang straight away went to the cash counter and collected the amount. The manager was in his cabin and he was made unconscious using a spray.

Before leaving the bank, the gang, using a spray, made the security guard and a few others also unconscious, leaving no one to report to the police.

With the loot, the gang took to their heels. Jackey, without anyone's notice, rang up to Veeru Dada and informed him about the route they were fleeing. When the gang entered a way through the forest, the gang of Veeru Dada pounced upon them and snatched the bag that contained the amount from the Chakrapani's gang. Before they were leaving, they removed the mask to *disclose* their identity.

It was like a thunderbolt for the gang of Chakrapani to learn that they were cleverly fooled by their *arch* rival, Veeru Dada and his gang.

Great was the joy of Veeru Dada and his gang when they saw the booty. They had a big celebration.

When Chakrapani came to know how Veeru Dada had fooled them, he was mad with rage.

"How dare a silly mouse to challenge a tiger? I will deal with that stupid fellow later on. But how did they come to know our operation which was planned out so secretly and confidently?" Chakrapani screamed at his gang. "I doubt whether someone from my gang betrayed this tiger."

"But boss, who will dare to do so?" Salim asked while casting his eyes on every one.

"That's what I want to know. If anyone has turned a spy for Veeru Dada, that fellow will be dealt with in a befitting manner!" Chakrapani cast his suspicious eyes on every one.

"I can't believe that any one has such guts, boss," said Jackey firmly.

"Jackey, you are my strongest aid. I appoint you to find out how the secret was leaked out."

"Yes, boss, I'll carry out your order *meticulously*." There was resolution in his words, but he hid his fear very cleverly.

Salim didn't like the compliment Chakrapani gave to Jackey, because he had considered himself more capable than Jackey and there was always a kind of competition among the duo to prove their worth.

"From now on, all of you need to be more *vigilant*." Chakrapani was very upset and cautioned them. "Now disperse." Jackey and Salim looked at each other like rivals and moved away.

18

Jim visits his own family secretly

Jim, the Super Kid, now thought about his own home. Jim remained back at his new home, but his other self, Super Kid, reached his previous home and remained there invisible. He wanted to know the happenings there.

It was morning time. He saw, Mrs. Clara Stephen, his 'step mother,' sitting on a sofa with her legs crossed in front of a large LED smart TV, sipping tea and watching a popular serial.

A maid was cooking food. The house was renovated and it had all amenities - A.C., music system, automatic-washing machine, food processor, refrigerator, and many other things of comfort. While watching the TV, she was also busy with chatting on her latest smart phone!

After some time Jim saw Uncle Sam entering the room.

"Where the hell, were you old fellow? I had told you to start my car and call me at the earliest. Hadn't I told you that my friend was waiting for me in the women's club?" She screamed at him and in a fit of fury threw the remaining hot tea on his face.

"The car was ready. As I was about to start the car, Sir called me. I was talking with him on the phone." Uncle Sam said without getting disturbed and wiped his face with his hands. It showed that he was used to such ill treatment!

Jim couldn't stand the arrogance and the rudeness of Clara. To him it was extremely shocking and he became furious. He wanted to teach the woman a lesson, but then he remembered the words of the angel not to take revenge. He controlled his anger.

Uncle Sam went out and started the car. Clara got into the car and away they went to the women's club.

Next Jim wanted to check where John was. He recalled how he too used to harass him and Jane. John used to be taken to the school in a car while Jim and Jane had to walk. Both of them were not allowed to sit at the dining table along with Stephen and his family. Whenever special dishes were prepared, John used to gulp them down, without leaving anything for Jim and Jane.

One day when Jim and Jane were coming down the steps from the terrace, John hid behind and suddenly stretched his leg, causing the duo to fall down. Both went rolling down and they sustained head injury. John came out from his hiding and *jeered* at them.

Stephen and his wife came to know that John had caused the accident but didn't even scold John for the same. They *pampered* him a lot and did not take interest in reforming him.

Jim just touched his forehead where there was a small scar. It reminded him the prank John had played on them.

Now Jim found John sitting with his friend, Raju, in an internet cafe and enjoying an 'adult stuff' instead of attending his classes.

Jim stood behind the duo and caused terrible strain in their eyes, by which they couldn't watch the screen. They wiped their eyes and glued to the screen again, but the view was blurred. They called up a man from the café, but the man found nothing wrong with the screen.

"No problem with the monitor. Go and check your eyes," the man said.

"We have paid money for one hour, but we could watch it only for ten minutes. Give us our money back," John shouted at the man. Fee was taken in advance in that café.

"We don't give back money here. There is no problem with our system. Both get out from here," the man was firm.

"You don't know who I am. No one dares to behave with me like this!" John pointed out his finger to the man threateningly. His friend tried to pacify John, but to no avail.

"I am the only son of Stephen, the owner of Trinity enterprises! I will be the next owner."

"Oh, I've heard about that cheat, I'm not scared! Do what you want, but just now CLEAR OUT!"

"How dare you buffoon, to order me. Take this from me." John gave a severe punch on his nose and blood oozed out. The man was about to fall but he held a table and stood upright. He wiped his face with his kerchief, then caught hold of John and held both his hands behind. Seeing that the situation was going out of control, John's friend *took to his heels*.

Meanwhile the man's assistant came back from outside and called up a police.

"Leave me, or you will regret." John kept saying.

Jim could have helped John but he thought that John had to learn a lesson.

The police came and found out that he was from the Navjyoti School, nearby. The police took John to his school.

The principal called Stephen and reported the incident. Stephen asked the policeman not to charge any case against his son and offered a bribe to the policeman.

The principal rusticated John for two days, for *bunking* the class and for fighting with the man in the café.

John didn't go home. He stayed with his friend and both enjoyed drugs and watched porn on his laptop.

When Super Kid saw that both the boys were watching 'the adult stuff', he wanted to teach them a lesson. Whenever they were browsing for such stuff, they could only find inspirational videos.

"What's happening? How come such videos on my laptop? I haven't downloaded them!" John was shocked and surprised.

His friend Raju *shrugged* his shoulders, "That's what puzzles me too. Something strange thing is happening with us! In the internet café also we had a *queer experience!*"

Irritated and disappointed, the boys shut down the laptop.

Suddenly Super Kid appeared in front of them. They were *taken aback* by the sudden *apparition.*

"Hey, who ...... who are you?" John *stammered.*

"I am known as Super Kid, a friend of the good ones and a terror to the trouble makers!"

"I........I had heard about you. But I could never believe in such nonsense stuff!" Raju said.

"Now can you believe, as you have seen me? I will give you something now so that you will remember me especially when you do any wrong things. This punishment is for some of your serious offences, such as, fighting with the man in the internet café, bunking classes and watching dirty videos!"

Super Kid sent his baton which began to beat the boys mercilessly for some time. Both started crying and then the baton disappeared and so did Super Kid.

Next, Jim wanted to find out about Stephen, the villain, who was responsible for the misery of his family.

19

Super Kid in Stephen's office

Super Kid saw Stephen sitting on the Managing Director's chair in the office of 'Trinity Enterprises'. It was previously occupied by his father. Super Kid stood in front of Stephen the intruder, invisible to everyone. On the table was kept the name of the new MD, Stephen Charles! He noticed sadly that his father's photo had been removed from the wall. To his horror, he also observed Stephen signing the office documents as he had already got power of attorney forcefully from his father. The memory of his loving parents tortured him and he wept silently.

Soon he regained his calmness and decided to make Stephen aware of the crimes committed by him.

Super Kid began to rotate the chair where Stephen was sitting. The chair went on revolving at a great speed and Stephen was shocked by this unusual happening and started yelling: "Hey, who is it? Stop! I say STOP!!"

Slowly his chair started rising in the air.

"THUD!"

The chair fell and Stephen was thrown away with his face down. He got hurt badly.

"What's going on? Who's it? I'll kill you, you devil!"

He looked around and to his great shock, couldn't see anyone.

Then Super Kid appeared in front of him.

Again Stephen yelled: "WHO ….who the hell are you? How did you appear from nowhere?"

"I am known as Super Kid! You don't deserve to be on this chair. This company is not yours. You have played foul and forcefully got the company in your name. You are an intruder!"

Then super Kid told him all that he knew about Stephen. "Hey, who are you? How do you know all these things?"

"I have super natural powers! My mission is to correct and punish the guilty and protect the good ones. This much is for the time being."

Super Kid vanished. Stephen sat with horror in his eyes. Sweat began to flow down from his body, though the room had air conditioning!

Super Kid wanted to know how his parents had died, whether they died in accidents or were murdered. He thought of Angel Shalom and lo! She stood in front of him! He was overjoyed to meet the divine messenger again.

"What do you want me to do for you, dear kid?" the angel asked lovingly.

"I suspect foul play by my step-father behind the death of my own parents. Is it true?" Super Kid enquired eagerly.

"Time has not yet come to reveal the truth. You are endowed with super-natural powers. Using it, you will slowly find out the truth behind. Don't take revenge, but leave it to God and let the law take its own course. Stay here for some time and you will come to know a number of things. God is pleased with your service to the needy ones and he has given you some more powers, by using them you will be able to help others and bust criminals and their evil plans. You haven't misused any of your powers so far, which makes you eligible to do more wonderful things. Continue doing good deeds and be helpful to others. *Adieu!*"

The angel disappeared from his sight. Super Kid now wanted to know the truth. He waited there invisible.

As he was watching, he saw a well-built Sardarji entering Stephen's office.

"Hey, who are you, man?" Stephen looked up and asked in a *hoarse* voice.

The stranger bolted the door and stood in front of him.

Stephen was about to press the calling bell. The stranger stopped him from taking such a step and said, "Look at me carefully before you call your attendants!" He removed his *turban*. To his surprise and shock, Super Kid noticed that the stranger was none other than Veeru Dada, the gang leader, from the slum! It was Veeru Dada who had made fun of the Cheer up India club members when they were cleaning the area there.

"Oh, it's you, Veeru! I couldn't recognize you. Even the police wouldn't recognize you in this *attire*!"

Veeru Dada was invited to take his seat. Stephen leaned forward and asked Veeru Dada, "Has anyone noticed you entering here?"

"Not at all, boss. My name is in the criminal records but the people here may not recognize me. I am not that popular, you see." Veeru Dada *chuckled*. "Besides, 'my fancy dress' helps me to hide my real identity wherever I go!" Veeru Dada laughed at his own joke.

Stephen looked upset and nervous.

"You look, worried. Is there any problem, boss?"

"Have you heard about a Super Kid?"

"Super Kid? Did that damn child come here also?"

"Someone claiming Super kid appeared suddenly, made my chair to revolve fast, then lifted it up and dropped it suddenly making me fall and get hurt. Still my head is spinning!"

"Oh, I see. Even I have had a taste of his baton which beat me up very badly. If ever I happen to meet him I'll definitely KILL him!"

"I don't feel like believing such stuff!" He leaned forward and said in a whisper. " But I can't forget my *encounter* with him either."

"I had assigned you a serious task some time back

to *eliminate* Vincent, the real owner of this company, which you had carried out successfully, without leaving any evidence. Now that the real owners of the company, Vincent and Annie, are dead, I am assigning you one more job – find out whether their children, Jim and Jane are alive and if so, I want to know their *whereabouts*! They had run away from here."

Super Kid was shocked and furious to know that his father was murdered by the evil plan designed by his step - father and it was executed by Veeru Dada!

"It's good that he has run away. Why to bother about him?" Veeru Dada enquired.

"The company's ownership is in Jim's name and as long as he is alive, I am only a caretaker. Murdering him in another accident and sending him to his parents is quite simple job for us, but I'm worried whether it will make me a suspect. I am scared about SP Vikram. He is an upright man who wouldn't take any bribe. I think time has not yet come to murder the child, but we must know where he is!"

"I will do the job for you, but I must get my advance just now."

"Haven't I paid you handsomely last time? You can trust me. Take fifty thousand in advance and the remaining amount after you bring me the happy news. Agreed?"

"Okay, boss. Keep remembering me and I will continue doing any job for you. To keep the secret, occasionally I will need some incentives, you see. As long as you share some of your earnings with this poor man and make me a wealthy man, I will *keep mum* about the murders. If any time you foolishly think about getting rid of me, you will land behind the bars!"

"You fool, don't dare to threaten me. I don't like such language. You don't know me well. If an ordinary man, a *vagabond*, could now occupy the seat of the Managing Director of such a flourishing company, and in fact become the owner of it, you can guess my abilities! I am a very clever and shrewd man. Anyway, let us be helpful to each other and that will be good for both of us! Now take the amount and *disperse*."

Veeru Dada, wore his turban again and left the office, carrying the amount in his bag. The memory of his parents *tormented* Super Kid. Was there any criminal conspiracy behind his mother's death? Was it an accident or murder? Now Jim wanted to find out the truth.

20

Super Kid investigates a murder mystery

Super Kid now followed Veeru Dada, in an invisible manner. When the criminal reached a lonely place, Super Kid sent his baton to beat him up. Veeru Dada swirled in great pain. He could only see the baton and it scared him all the more. He remembered the similar experience he had in the slum and soon realized that he was encountering the powerful Super Kid again! He shuddered at the thought.

"Please spare me, it's paining terribly!" Veeru Dada cried like a child.

"You, wicked man, tell me how did you kill the owners of 'Trinity Enterprises'?"

"I will tell you everything, please stop beating me." Super Kid now showed himself.

"Okay, I shall stop now. Tell me about it in detail."

"Stephen had given me a quotation to kill Vincent sir. Accordingly I waited for an opportunity. One day I noticed Vincent sir driving his own car alone. When he reached a lonely place, I drove a truck and hit his car from behind. The car was pushed down and it fell into a deep valley. I saw it blasting down in the *ravines*! I reported it to Stephen sir and he was extremely happy."

Super Kid wept bitterly. He could almost feel the agony that his loving father went through. He was silent for some time, trying to suppress his deep emotions.

"Where did you get the truck?" Super Kid asked him after sobbing for some time.

"I had stolen it and removed the number plate. I pushed the truck down into the deep valley and destroyed the evidence. The police thought that it was just an accident and closed the matter."

"How cruel of you to commit such a crime! How did you kill his wife?"

"It was also in the same way. But she was not killed by me. One day she was going to the church. When she was returning alone, Stephen sir used a tempo to create the 'accident'! It was not the first time he killed someone!! His wife was also involved in the conspiracy."

For some time Jim couldn't talk at all. "So it was my step father who murdered my loving mother and this villain who had killed my father!" Jim muttered to himself with mixed feelings of rage, bitterness and despair. The memory of his beloved parents filled his eyes with tears. The news about the sad end of his parents was so agonizing that he couldn't speak for a long time.

"Wasn't there any police enquiry?" After managing to control his emotions, Jim asked.

Police sub-inspector, Shankar Das was in charge of the police station, then. Stephen sir bribed him and the matter was settled as an accident.

Jim was lost in thoughts and was mum for some time. Veeru Dada thought that Super Kid had gone away and he took to his heels. Soon the baton appeared again in front of him and showered a number of thrashing.

Super Kid snatched the bag of money away from the criminal.

"Please give back my bag. If you want, beat me some more time but don't take away my money."

"You don't deserve the amount as you have got it by doing criminal activities. You must do honest work to earn a living. This amount will be given to an orphanage!"

Super Kid had recorded the confession of Veeru Dada and hoped that it would help the police in finding evidence against the criminals.

Veeru Dada went home a broken man.

Super Kid dropped the bag containing the amount inside an orphanage. He left a chit saying that the amount was donated by a well - wisher who wanted to remain unknown.

Super Kid felt a sense of satisfaction as never before for bringing cheer to the inmates. He said to himself, "Now I have experienced that real happiness lies in making others happy".

Stephen's encounter with 'the ghost of Vincent'

Next, Super Kid appeared in Stephen's office once again. He wanted to teach the villainous character one more lesson.

Stephen was busy, checking some files. Super Kid sat on a chair opposite to him and assumed the form of Vincent, his late father.

Stephen was *immersed* in his work for some time, and then he lifted up his head.

At the same time the lights went off. Suddenly there was a deafening sound of lightning and thundering.

Stephen was frozen at the sudden turn of events. He *leaped* from his chair and was about to scream but no sound came from his throat.

He wondered as how the lights went off suddenly and where the lightning and thunder came from when the sky was clear so far.

He fell into the chair and tried desperately to press the call button but there was no electricity!

Suddenly there was one more lightning and he saw a figure sitting on a chair in front of him!

He yelled in shock and fear because nobody had entered the room.

Suddenly lights came and he saw that the figure resembled Vincent sir!! His eyes bulged at the sight.

"Oh! It's a Ghost!!" Stephen leaped from his chair as if he got an electric shock. He was shivering from head to toe. Sweat streamed down on his face, though the room had air cooler.

"WHO.....who are ......you?" Stephen stammered in shock and fear.

"Don't you know me, Stephen Charles, the intruder, the *traitor*, the killer and what not?" Super Kid's voice sounded like thundering.

"Am I, dreaming? It's......it's NOT possible!" Words chocked in his throat.

"Why isn't it possible? Because you had got me killed with the help of Veeru Dada, hadn't you?"

"How come that I am speaking with a ghost? I ....I can't believe it." Stephen *sputtered*.

"Then take this," Super Kid sent his baton which began to shower beatings upon Stephen. The baton came from nowhere and Stephen tried to catch hold of it, but his hands got hurt very badly. The criminal now began to run here and there inside the room. He tried to run out of the room, but in vain. Super Kid, who had assumed the image of Vincent, blocked his way.

"Please stop this nonsense; I can't stand it any longer!" Stephen groaned. The baton stood still.

"This is nothing at all, Stephen. Do you know how much it hurt as I was hit by the truck and I fell into the valleys? As my head hit on rocks, blood streamed down from my aching body, my bones were broken and eyes damaged! Just imagine the agony and the excruciating pain I had to suffer, the last pangs and the horror I experienced! Is your pain anything in comparison with my agony?"

"I don't know. Still I can't believe that I am speaking with a ghost, the ghost of my boss, Vincent sir!"

"When you came to me for help, I appointed you as an accountant in my company. And then what did you do? You cheat, forged my account, began to steal money and when I dismissed you from my company, you took revenge on me! You had got power of attorney from me forcefully and by misusing it, became the boss of my own company You got me killed in an accident and then forcefully married my wife, for money!"

Super Kid watched the expression on Stephen's face, who couldn't believe that he was talking to a ghost. He sat there sweating.

"You killed my dear wife! Being tired of the ill treatment by all your family members, my only son, Jim, ran away. After some days my daughter Jane also escaped from the torture by your wife. Is this the way to respond for being a benefactor to you? Is this the way to repay for the goodness shown by me? What an ungrateful creature you are!!"

"You are right. I had to get you killed with the help of Veeru Dada and I killed your wife myself! But how am I talking to a ghost? I think I will go crazy."

Stephen grasped for breath. After some time he continued, "I too wanted to become rich. My wife encouraged me to take such steps. There was no other way to achieve our goal."

"By *treachery* and by murder, you have become rich! But you have no right to use this property, as what's not earned by hard work, is not yours. You have to pay for the crime you have committed! You are not going to sleep peacefully hereafter."

The ghost disappeared, so also did Super Kid. Stephen experienced a *conglomeration* of feelings –fear, doubts, confusion, uncertainty, horror! He gasped for breath and sank into his chair.

Stephen, the hard hearted criminal, had still no *remorse*! He was a criminal to the core!!

22

Super Kid teaches John a lesson

Jim as Super Kid followed John wherever he went. John had treated both Jim and Jane very cruelly by playing various pranks upon them.

Jim recalled how both were punished severely for a prank played by John. One day Clara, john's mother, went out for a shopping but had forgotten to lock her cupboard in which she used to keep her ornaments. John was looking for such an opportunity and he stole two gold chains and hid one in Jane's school bag and another in the pocket of Jim's short pant.

When Clara came back after her shopping, to her shock she realized that she had forgotten to lock the cupboard. She immediately opened the inner secret locker to make sure that her ornaments were safe, but found two of her gold chains missing!

She ran out of the room in panic and yelled out, "All of you come here at once!"

It was evening time and all the children were in their

rooms. They came running, thinking that something terrible thing had happened.

"Tell me who has stolen my gold chain?" The woman glared at the children *furiously*.

"We have not taken it," Jim told her innocently.

"Who asked you to speak for all? Tell me, did you take it?" she screamed.

"No, mom. I was washing the plates in the kitchen."

"What about you, Jane? Why did you take my gold chain? Speak the truth or I'll tear you to pieces!"

"I haven't seen your chain, mom. I'll never steal." Jane *trembled* like a rose leaf.

"Then how come it is missing? Has it flown away or has it melted and vanished?"

John stood there acting very innocently and suggested, "Mom, why don't you check all their bags? You can check mine also."

"That's a good idea, dear. You are indeed a smart boy!" She patted him for the suggestion and immediately began to search their bags. John also voluntarily undertook the search.

"Here, look! One of the thieves is caught!!" she called out as she held the chain which was found in Jane's bag.

Jane and Jim stood frozen with fear. John clapped his hands merrily.

"Let me check now the other fellow's bag." She didn't find anything there.

Meanwhile John checked the pocket of Jim's pants and screamed: "Mom I have found the other missing chain!"

Jim and Jane were shocked again and felt miserable. They knew that it was John's prank.

"You, thieves, how dare you steal MY ornaments?"

The woman was mad with fury and caught hold of both the children and began to *flog* them with a broom. She slapped them and pushed them against a wall and shook them violently.

"We have not taken your chain," the children kept on telling her but the woman was not ready to listen to them. While they cried bitterly, John kept on jeering at them.

Just then Stephen returned from his office. When he came to know about the missing chain, he also beat them with a cane, until it broke. Uncle Sam watched the plight of the children, felt sympathy for the kids but he was helpless. He was sure that they would never steal.

After some time, John went into his room and told his friend, Raju, over his mobile about the prank played by him. That time Clara, while passing that way, overheard him and the truth was revealed to her. She later on told Stephen that they were misled by John, but they were not at all sorry for beating the innocent children. Moreover they didn't even scold John for the prank played by him.

On the day when they were discussing about it, Uncle Sam heard it and reported to Jim.

"Dear Jim, both sir and madam have come to know that the stealing *episode* was a prank played by John. He had stolen the chains and kept them with both of you so that you will get beaten. You were punished for no fault of yours. I feel so sorry."

"I had guessed that it was his doing. But what could we do?"

"In spite of knowing the truth, they didn't even question John about it, they just kept quiet! In fact, they are spoiling their own son, by not correcting him," Uncle Sam said.

When Jim recalled the incident, his eyes were filled with tears.

Now Jim returned to the present from the painful past memory. Jim found John and his friend, Raju, sitting in a park one evening. He listened to their talk.

"Are you ready for the forthcoming exam?" Raju asked John.

"Ready? Who's interested in the exams? But some way we have to manage to pass to the next class."

"By now all the question papers are typed and kept in the office locker. If we succeed in getting a copy each, we can easily pass and that too with high marks!"

"I know. But how's it possible?"

"I have thought about it. Tomorrow I will manage

to get an imprint of the office key on a piece of soap and then a duplicate key can be made," John's voice expressed confidence.

"I can get a spray by which we can make the watchman unconscious and then we shall steal the question papers which we need."

"Okay, then, we shall meet tomorrow."

The next day as planned out, both came to the school gate in the evening.

"Why are you here, boys? Go away and study for your exams," The security told them sternly.

"We came to show you something interesting, on the mobile," Raju told him. "It's about YOU!"

"Show," the security expressed curiosity to watch it.

As he was watching the screen, John used a spray. The man fell unconscious. Then both the boys looked around and after making sure that they were not being watched, climbed the wall and jumped down. The boys dragged the security and laid him behind a tree.

Immediately they rushed to the office, opened the office door and got inside.

Super Kid followed them, invisible.

Using the flashlight from their mobile, they managed to open the locker and searched for the question papers and finally managed to collect all the required ones. Both were very happy in their success.

Super Kid was waiting for this moment and he acted

promptly. He made the security wake up. The man noticed the light in the office and felt that something was fishy. He recalled how the boys were *pretending* to show something on their mobile and then he was not aware as what had happened.

He ran to the office and opened the door. To his horror he noticed the same boys inside.

The security put on the light. The boys were shocked to see him and looked at each other with fear. They tried to pounce upon him, but the security caught hold of them and tied them. He immediately rang up to the principal and reported the matter to him.

The principal called up Stephen and said: "I'm sorry to tell you, your son has become a headache for me."

"Head ache? What's the matter now?" Stephen asked with growing irritation.

"John and his friend broke into the school office in the night and tried to steal some question papers after making the security man unconscious."

"Oh, that's all! I thought something was very serious."

"It's not at all a silly matter. If he continues showing such tendencies, he may turn into a criminal in its true sense."

"Leave it sir. I have too many problems to deal with here in the office. You just scold him if you want, and forget about it. Boys are *boisterous* and mischievous, it's their nature. "

"If you are not willing to correct him, I may have to report to the police!"

"Hello, don't dare to threaten me, you don't know Stephen. You have a family, haven't you? Do you want your only son to return home safely?"

"Please, don't do any harm to him. As you say, I'll close the case after giving him a stern warning."

"That's like a wise man!" The call was cut from the other side.

"No wonder why the son has become such a troublesome one. As the father is, so is the son! With his father's support, the son may turn into a worse criminal!" The principal told to himself.

A chase

Jim as Super Kid went to his own home and wanted to know the happenings there. He remained invisible.

Clara, the wife of Stephen, was watching TV as usual and at the same time chatting on what's app!

John entered the hall and went to his mother. She lifted her eyes from the mobile and asked, "Yes, my dear, what do you want?"

"Mummy, give me ten thousand rupees," said John.

"What! Ten thousand rupees!! Why do you want so much?"

"I want to give a party to my friends."

"You want ten thousand rupees, just to give a party!"

"I know it's nothing for you. Last time you bought a sari for thirty thousand rupees! After all it's NOT our money!!"

"Don't question me. And don't talk so. Now you are only a child, a teenager of just fifteen years. You shouldn't spend so much money for a party. If you want, just take thousand bucks!"

"Thousand bucks! That's just tips we give to a waiter! No, I don't want your money."

John went into his room angrily and slammed the door.

"Hey, wait!" Clara shouted but John had already gone into his room.

Suddenly there was a call on her mobile. The person on the other side said, "I have brought the 'stuff' and am waiting outside your house."

"Just wait there. Is there anyone around there?" She asked.

"No madam, not a soul."

"That's good. Don't ring the bell, I am coming out."

She put off the phone, held it in her hand and opened the door quietly. A man handed her a small packet, she took it, hid it under her dress carefully, turned back, opened the door, got in, closed the door behind her, quietly went inside her room, opened her cupboard, kept the 'stuff', looked about her to make sure that nobody was around there, locked the secret locker and kept the key behind a flower vase. She left her mobile on the dressing table and went to the wash room. The TV was still on.

Now Super Kid pressed the call log button to find out whom she had contacted. He noted down the number.

Super Kid noticed John entering the room. John went near the wash room and listened. He could hear water pouring down from the shower and understood that his mother was taking bath. He returned, went slowly to the cupboard, found the key, opened it, took out the packet, removed two *sachets* and kept them in his pockets. Slowly he locked the cupboard and placed the key exactly in the same place. After assuring himself that no one had observed him, he went out quietly.

After half an hour, Clara came out, put on her best dress and wore some gold ornaments. She removed the packets and kept them in her bag. She looked like a society lady, dressed up in her best. She glanced at her watch, and went out. She got into her BMW and drove it away.

Super Kid followed her invisible to others.

She drove the car for about an hour, reached an isolated area, stopped the car and looked around. A young man came towards her on a sports bike, stopped near the car and stepped down from the bike. He said a few code words and she replied in code words, then she handed over the packets. The young man took the packets, counted the sachets, opened his brief case, removed a few bundles of notes and then handed them to the lady.

She glanced at the bundles and exclaimed, "Hello boy, the amount is less."

"You have given me two sachets less, madam!" said the young man still wearing his helmet.

"But I had counted and kept the sachets, how come they are less?"

"I don't know. That's your problem. I've paid for the stuff you have handed over to me."

"I'm confused! I had carefully locked the stuff in my cupboard and had gone to have a shower. Then I brought them with me. But where have the two sachets of drug gone!"

"It's a grave matter of concern. Someone had removed two sachets, which means you were being WATCHED!"

"Oh! Is it so......!" She shuddered at the thought. She remained quiet for some time and then recalled John demanding money.

"Could it be that my own son has stolen the packets? Or is it that driver Sam? " she asked herself and was overwhelmed by fear. After some time she enquired him: "By the by, what's your name?"

"You needn't know it. Anyway, there is no problem. You may call me Salim!"

"Salim, Chakrapani's aid! So my 'step mother' is involved in drug trafficking and is associated with the dreaded Don!" Super Kid said to himself and the truth made him frozen for a moment.

He acted immediately. He made both Clara and Salim frozen there. They tried to move but were shocked to learn that they were made statues!

Super Kid found SP Vikram and his team heading

towards the station. He whispered in his ears, "Super Kid is here next to you. Please take the small lane to your left side. I've made statues of two people involved in drug trafficking, you can take them into your custody. If you want to ask me anything, please switch on your mobile and pretend talking to somebody. I'll reply."

The SP did so. He cleared some of his doubts and then turned to the driver and said," Take the small lane next to your left side. I've got a message that two people are exchanging drugs!"

The driver drove the Scorpio and went towards the spot where Clara and Salim stood frozen, but to the police, they looked like talking to each other. Super Kid now released them and at once they noticed the speeding Scorpio and tried to flee. The police team pounced upon them and took them to their custody. One policeman took the BMW and another the bike and all went to the police station.

"Sir, you have never told us how you get such information," Sub inspector Shankar Das told SP Vikram.

The SP just smiled and said, "For security reasons, let it be a secret."

Then nobody dared to ask him any more questions.

All the three vehicles sped towards the police station.

Next Super Kid wanted to find out about John. John had gone out to meet his friend, Raju' near a river side. John took out some powder from a packet and both consumed it. After some time, John's friend snatched the other packet and began to run towards the main road. John ran after him with growing rage for being tricked.

Super Kid acted swiftly. He informed the SP that two boys were having drugs with them. Luckily, the SP and a few policemen were quite near the spot where the boys were fighting.

John ran after his friend at full speed and finally overpowered him. John showered blows after blows and blood started flowing from his nose. John lifted a large stone lying on the side of the road and was about to drop it on his friend's head.

Immediately they could hear the siren from the police vehicle. To their horror, they saw a Scorpio having a beacon with multiple colours running at great speed towards them.

"FREEZE, it's a police vehicle!" Raju screamed.

At once John dropped the stone on one side of the road and began to flee from the sight. Raju tried to run but he couldn't, as he had got hurt from the fighting. The Scorpio stopped near them and a policeman dragged Raju to the Scorpio. Two other policemen chased John for some time and finally caught him, gave a few slaps and took him also into the police vehicle.

Now all of them headed towards the police station.

24

Veeru Dada learns the identity of Super Kid

Durasar was a notorious Satan worshipper who had acquired some devilish power over the years. 'Durasar' was not his original name but an assumed one. His followers also had adopted different names. He had setup an 'Ashram', adopted his own style of functioning and had quite many followers.

He had heard that Super Kid was helping people and thereby glorifying God's name. He and his gang couldn't tolerate the humanitarian activities of Super Kid and they considered him as a dangerous rival.

"Whoever is this kid, he has to be put to death immediately. He is bringing glory to God through his helping nature. Our Master, the Satan, is infuriated by this kid's activities," said Durasar to his devilish disciples.

'But there is a serious problem – we don't know his true identity. He has lot of powers like appearing anywhere, that too, invisible, and sending his baton to beat up people," Durgun told his boss.

Durgun was his most faithful disciple and the mastermind behind many evil activities. These two were the most dreaded ones who were bent upon turning more and more devotees and spiritual people to accept Satan as their master.

"God is Satan's arch enemy as well as ours. Anything that brings glory to God, makes our Master *dejected* and *humiliated*", Durasar said in a sad tone. "We need to increase the number of our followers, the Satan – worshippers. People should stop going to the prayer houses, they must lose their faith in God, let the children disobey their parents, let them leave their studies and turn their attention to browse the internet. The social media is really helping us to get more and more youngsters turning to evil ways like watching *porn* sites and getting involved in crimes."

"The present time is much favourable for us, as more and more people are spending a lot of time with the social network rather than using their time for 'useful' activities, such as being with the family and spending time for prayer! Of course, we don't consider them as useful activities. Today's youngsters can't think about a life without mobile and internet!!" Durgun smiled.

"Many youngsters, even children, are turning away from God and are keen in following our great Master. They disobey their parents, watch the stuff meant for adults, skip their studies and prayer and while away their time. There is *tremendous* tension in many families. It's indeed good news for us. Family relationship is at stake as there are all sorts of abuses!" Andhera, another follower, smiled as he said.

"As time goes, we will be getting more and more people to follow our ways. Our Master is quite happy about the changed times. There are broken families where family members fight among themselves especially over property. We hear about corruption, theft, abuses murder and adultery; the list is unending. "

Durasar paused for some time and then continued, "Today, let us have a longer session of Satan Worship by which we may obtain more powers to destroy goodness and to add more evil activities. Let us do hope that our Great Master will guide us to trap Super Kid, in order to take away his super powers."

Soon a call was given and all the devotees of Satan assembled in the hall. Lights were put off. Only a dim light came from lanterns and candles.

The people who were present in the hall wore black dresses. A long table was laid in the centre which was covered with a black sheet. There were posters on the walls that *depicted* images of Satan and a large statue of Lucifer was kept on the centre. An image of star with Satan's image inserted also was seen in the room.

Durasar, the chief priest, wore a red coloured long robe and his face was covered with a mask having the image of Satan. The worshippers shouted after Durasar, "Come Satan, the king of Darkness, fill us with your power. May your followers increase to spread evil in the world. Let people fight and shed their blood which will *appease* your thirst for blood. Let God be ignored, despised and humiliated! Let people worship Satan and not God!!"

The worship continued for some time. Then Durasar told the gathering: "Our Master has revealed to me now that if more and more people join our group, he will shower on us a lot of power and wealth. The more we deny God, the more our Master will be pleased with us."

Super Kid, who was present there, could not tolerate the *blasphemy*. He sent a powerful *hurricane* which blew away the images of Satan. The black dress, which the Satan worshippers had worn, and the black cloth, spread on the table in the centre, caught fire and the room was filled with smoke.

The worshippers were stunned by the sudden happenings. There was terror in every eye. Then Super Kid's voice thundered in the hall.

"You have forgotten your God, who has created you and has taken care of you till this moment by His Divine providence. He is a forgiving God who is kind, merciful and all goodness. Instead of worshipping Him you are worshipping the Devil, God's arch enemy, the king of lies! Ask God's forgiveness, otherwise His *wrath* will destroy you!" Super Kid's voice *reverberated* in the hall.

"Hey, who are you? How dare you speak like that? We don't have faith in God. We believe in Satan, our Master. He is all powerful and almighty!" Durasar yelled. "Show yourself, if you dare!"

"Look! I'm here! You can't do anything to me because the most powerful God is with me. He has granted me some divine power!"

They saw his image near the door. Durgun hurled an iron rod at him, but it didn't hit him. Super Kid vanished but appeared in another place. The worshippers began to throw stones at him, but he disappeared and appeared elsewhere. The game went on for some time. Finally all of them were tired of their futile effort.

All were shocked and sad at the unexpected happenings. Then they *resumed* Satan worship, with fear in their hearts. Durasar was leading the worship.

When he finished the worship, a man in black came in and whispered something in Durasar's ears.

"Okay friends. Keep on worshipping Satan. I will be back after some time. I have a visitor," Durasar said and left the hall.

Durasar met the visitor, who introduced himself as Veeru Dada.

"Okay Veeru, what can I do for you?" Durasar enquired.

"I am sure that you have heard about Super Kid. I want to find out his identity." Veeru Dada leaned forward and told Durasar.

"Heard about him! He is our bitterest enemy, enemy NUMBER ONE! He was here just now and has *ransacked* our place of worship."

"Then we have the same one as our enemy. He had flogged me severely and I will never forget his blows and the humiliation!"

"Regarding his identity........let me see. I will ask my Master, the Satan, to reveal his identity to me. Yes. It's a good idea. If we know who is hiding behind that mask, we can kill him easily. But how come, he has got such super natural powers, I wonder."

"Your Master may reveal that too."

"You wait here for some time, let me worship him some more time and when he is pleased with me, I will ask him about it."

"Okay. I can wait for some more time."

Durasar went to his private room and worshipped the Satan. After some time the lights went off. There was a thundering sound and then a dark horrible looking figure appeared. His husky voice thundered in the room: "Yes, Durasar, my dear, what do you want from me?"

"I, your humble servant, desire to know the identity of Super Kid, your majesty."

"I, the prince of Darkness, am pleased with your devotion to me. So I'll reveal the secret to you. There is a kid named Jim who is the son of Vincent and Anne. You do not know his family, but tell Veeru Dada who will be too happy to know his identity. Super Kid is none other than this kid named Jim."

"Thank you, your Majesty. How did he get such power?"

"I am not permitted to tell you that. "

"Where can we find Jim?"

"He is a student at Green Valley English Medium School, run by one Iqbal. He and his sister, Jane, are living at Victor's family. For the time being, this much information will be sufficient for you."

Again there was a thundering sound and the Devil vanished!

Durasar came out of the room and informed Veeru Dada immediately.

"WHAT? Jim is the Super Kid!! I can hardly believe it. I know him very well. Any way, thank you, sir."

"Keep the 'thanks' with you. I demand my reward for revealing the truth."

"Reward? How much is your amount?"

"Not much. Only five lakhs!"

"FIVE LAKHS just for disclosing a single secret!"

"Not just one secret, you fool. I've told you three secrets – first one about the identity of Super Kid, the second, about his sister and the third, where to locate them. I expect to get the amount within two days. Or else, I will offer your blood to my Master!"

"Oh, no! I am doing this mission for another person. I have to consult him."

"Do whatever damn thing you want to do. What I need is cash, nothing but CASH!"

"I will meet you tomorrow, with the amount!"

"Okay, that will be good for you. You may leave now!"

Immediately Veeru Dada rang up to Stephen: "Sir, You had asked me to find out the whereabouts of Jim. I have found it out from a mighty person having supernatural powers. He has demanded ten lakhs as reward."

"What? Ten lakhs! That's too much."

"If the money is not paid to him by tomorrow, he will kill both of us."

"You fool, why did you *drag* my name into it? You should have only told your name."

"Don't play over smart, sir. You don't mind if I'm killed! You want to be safe! It won't work, sir. I'm not a fool!"

"Now first tell me where is Jim."

"Again you want to be over smart, sir. First arrange the amount and then you will hear the secret from me, not just one secret but three. You will be excited to hear the secrets!"

"Ten lakhs! Don't you think it's too much?"

"I don't think so. What's more important, our lives or money? After all it's not YOUR money!"

"Now don't talk anything more over the phone. It's not safe. Come to my office by twelve o'clock tomorrow, tell me the secret and take the amount. I will call you back tomorrow as soon as the cash is ready."

Stephen disconnected the phone.

Veeru Dada smiled. "You are a smart guy, Veeru,"

Veeru Dada appreciated himself. "Five lakhs for Durasar and another five lakhs for you, great Don Veeru Dada! Ha! Ha!" Veeru was excited about his easily earned fortune.

"I've already got fifty thousand as token money and he may give me a lakh more at least, for revealing three great secrets," he thought.

Veeru Dada, however, knew very little what was in store for him.

25

Jim and Super Kid found missing!

Veeru Dada's two great aids, Virendra and Vittal, were still in the jail as they were caught red handed by the police for selling drugs to the boys. Veeru Dada's several attempts to get them released, turned futile as they were caught by the Anti-Narcotics Cell.

Now he had another two strong aids – Divakar and Shankar. One day Veeru Dada called both of them and told them about his plan, "Now we know the identity of Super Kid. He is none other than a child from 'Green Valley School'. If we succeed in capturing him, we don't have to be scared about him anymore."

"What will we be doing with the child after catching him?" Divakar enquired.

"As soon as the child comes in our hand, we will make him unconscious. Otherwise he may use his power and escape," said Veeru Dada.

"Why not kill him at once?" Shankar asked.

"That's risky. Besides, I want to take revenge on him

for beating me with his damn baton. I want to tell him that I've learnt his identity and then I want to see his miserable condition. I want to enjoy his face turning pale. Let us get him in our place. The Kid has got some sort of supernatural power, so we have to be extra vigilant and cautious. After our successful operation I'll demand a huge amount from Stephen, because he wanted to kill this boy so that he could become the real boss of the company."

Then Veeru Dada explained to them his plan of operation. As per the plan, the trio went to the Green Valley School, in the afternoon. It was about two o'clock and the school was just over. There were school buses, rickshaws and private vehicles waiting for the children.

The gang stood outside the school, waiting for Jim to come out. Veeru Dada could recognize Jim because he was the leader of the Cheer up India club which did a commendable work of cleaning up the slum where he was hiding then.

Now Veeru Dada saw Jim coming out with three more children, but he wanted only Jim.

The gang burst something and cleverly produced a thick smoke screen. Suddenly, they caught hold of Jim, made him unconscious using chloroform, carried the child, got into their vehicle and hastened to their destination.

Everything took place within seconds and no one knew what was going on. The children cried aloud. When the smoke got cleared, Jim was found missing!

Jerry, Marina and Jane were shocked and turned pale! They began to cry aloud asking for help. Some of the staff members and children came running and enquired why they were crying. They told them about Jim's missing. All were alarmed and disturbed. Someone informed the principal, Mrs. Susan, about the incident. She was very much upset and rushed to the outside gate.

The children narrated the sudden unfortunate incident and continued crying. The Principal reported the matter to SP Vikram and also informed Victor. The SP and his team immediately began to search for Jim. The family of Victor was taken aback and was in utter misery because Jim was so dear to them. Jane cried bitterly and no words could console her.

Now Veeru Dada and his gang took Jim straight to their hide-out. Jim woke up after some time but couldn't figure out as what had happened.

He opened his eyes and saw Veeru Dada. The criminal just smiled *sarcastically*.

"Open your eyes, Jim, no, the great SUPER KID!" Veeru Dada said sardonically. "Now we know your identity and you are finished! Super Kid! BAH! You and your baton!! I'll flog you to death!"

Jim heard his words and was taken aback. He recalled the Angel's words not to reveal his identity to anyone. Using his divine power he thought immediately, "May all those who know my identity instantly forget it!" At once, Veeru Dada, two of his gang members and Durasar forgot the identity of Super Kid.

At the same time Veeru Dada sprayed a *sedative* by which Jim fell unconscious again.

"Who brought this child here?" Veeru Dada enquired.

"We don't know, boss. We thought you had brought him," Shankar said.

"I haven't. Anyway, throw him into a chamber. We can make use of him for stealing money," the Don remarked.

Accordingly the gang threw him into a chamber. They kept on wondering as how he came into their hide-out and the matter remained a *puzzle* in their mind!

26

Attempts to recapture Chakrapani

To SP Vikram, the escape of Chakrapani and his gang from the jail was like a bolt from the above. The missing of Jim was another shock for him. He tried to call Super Kid, but in vain. He was shocked, desperate and disturbed as why Super Kid didn't appear before him. He suspected that something had happened to him.

One day he was sitting in his room, upset and lost in deep thought. Sarita, his wife, asked him the reason for his worry.

"You look very much depressed, what's the matter?"

"The same thing, the most notorious criminal Chakrapani and his gang have escaped again from the jail!"

"Oh, no! But how did they manage again?"

SP Vikram narrated the incident.

"Why don't you contact Super Kid? I'm sure he will help you to capture him again."

"Do you think that I didn't try?"

"But didn't he help you?"

"He has not appeared to me this time; I fear something has gone wrong."

"My god, that's very disturbing. What might have happened to him? He is Super Kid, and not an ordinary child. I don't think anyone can do harm to him as he has supernatural powers. Definitely something serious thing has happened."

"The worst thing is, we don't know anything about his whereabouts. We don't know who he is, where he stays, and how he appears suddenly and so on. Now that we can't expect his help, our team will have to find out the criminal gang. Besides, a kid from Green Valley School is also missing!"

"Oh, NO!"

SP Vikram decided to *intensify* his search for the dreaded gang. He and his team made a thorough enquiry in the jail where the gang was kept and realized that the guard, Sharma, had a hand in the escape. Sharma's absence from his duty added to his *suspicion* about him.

The jail superintend gave Vikram all the details of Sharma. Immediately, the team rushed to Sharma's home. The police vehicle, Scorpio, stopped in front of the house. A policeman knocked at the door.

Mrs. Sharma opened the door. She was shocked to find a policeman standing in front of the door. She also noticed a police vehicle parked nearby.

"Where is Sharma? Why has he not reported to duty?" The policeman asked her in a stern voice.

Mrs. Sharma stammered, "He ……. he told me that he was going to his duty as usual and he went in the morning, two days back. We came to know that he hadn't attended his duty. We are deeply worried about him."

"Don't act smart. He has not gone for his duty. I am sure that you have heard already that Chakrapani and his gang have escaped from the jail, the day before yesterday. We have got proof that your husband had helped the gang and so we are looking for the criminals. Come on, tell me where is Sharma?"

"Oh, my god! I don't believe that my husband will do such a crime, helping a gang of criminals to escape. I am telling the truth that I don't know where he is. He has not told me anything. Actually we had gone yesterday to the Jail Superintend to enquire about my husband."

"Who else is in the house?"

"We have only one son. He has already gone to the school."

"What is his name? In which school is he studying?"

"His name is Ravi. He is studying in the seventh class at Green Valley English Medium School."

"Where is Sharma's mobile phone?"

"He has taken it along."

"Why are you so sure about it?"

"That's because he had forgotten to take the phone. I had brought it and given to him."

Without telling anything more, the constable went to the police vehicle and passed the information to SP Vikram. The officer asked some of the policemen to have a thorough checking in the house. But they could find neither Sharma nor could obtain any clue.

"Let us go to the school where Sharma's son is studying." Vikram was a little disappointed.

SP Vikram went to the Principal's room. She was in the office.

"Sir, please take your seat." Mrs. Susan said very politely. "May I know the reason for your visit?"

"Is a child named Ravi Sharma studying in your school?"

"Oh, yes. He is in the seventh class. Has he committed some….."

"Oh, no, it's nothing of that sort. His father is a guard in the jail and he has not attended to his duty today. We checked in his home, but he is not found there. His wife doesn't know where he has gone. I want to question Ravi whether he knows anything about his father."

Mrs. Susan rang the bell and a peon appeared near the door.

"Call Ravi Sharma from seventh class, immediately."

"Okay, madam."

"Is there any serious issue, sir? What has Ravi's father done?"

"We are suspecting that he has helped a *notorious* gang to escape from the jail."

"You mean Chakrapani and his gang?"

"That's right. I know that it's the breaking news these days!"

Just then Ravi appeared at the principal's room. He looked upset as he was called into her room.

"Come in Ravi. This police officer wants to ask you something. Don't worry. Just tell him the truth." Mrs. Susan spoke in a kind tone.

"Ravi, how many brothers and sisters do you have, son?" SP Vikram asked.

"I don't have any brother or sister. I am the only child."

"I see. So, you don't have any siblings. do you know where your father has gone?"

"He had told us that he was going for his duty and left home at the usual time. But he didn't return in the evening. So we are worried about him."

"Have you got any relatives around here?"

"No sir, they are in our native place in Uttar Pradesh. Is my father really missing, sir?" Ravi was getting disturbed.

"Oh, no, son. There's nothing serious. I just wanted to know why he has not reported to his duty. Okay, you may go now. Don't worry."

SP Vikram felt sorry for Ravi, who was almost of his son's age.

The police officer got up to go. "Okay madam. Thank you for your cooperation. I hope to find his father soon."

When the police officer went out, Mrs. Susan recalled the incident that had taken place during the school picnic on the previous year. Various events of the day flashed vividly on her mind's screen; the three boys - Abu, Tony and Ravi playing pranks on Vinay, Abu accidently falling into the swamp, Vinay saving him by risking his own life, Super Kid's sudden appearance and rescuing Vinay from being drowned........ Though Ravi was also a mischievous child, after the incident he had *turned over a new leaf.* She was concerned about Ravi.

SP Vikram went back to his office. He was determined to capture Chakrapani and his gang. He once again tried a desperate attempt to call Super Kid, but again there was no response. Now he realized that something serious thing had happened to him. He was at the end of his wits as how to find Super kid as he didn't know the kid's whereabouts.

While he was lost in his thought, the phone rang. He picked up the mobile. The Director General of Police was on the line.

"Vikram, have you got any clue about the whereabouts of Chakrapani and his gang?" The police officer asked anxiously.

"No, sir. Still we are trying our level best to trace them."

"What about the missing child?"

"Sorry sir, we couldn't find him yet."

"I am proud of your capability and credibility. I don't keep much trust on your subordinates and that's why I had asked you to deal with these cases; I am confident that you will be successful. Anyway, speed up with your enquiry, and report to me about its progress at the earliest."

"Definitely, sir. Thank you for the trust you have placed on me."

"Keep up your spirit."

SP Vikram was restless again. He called a few of his most trusted policemen and again went out looking for some hints as which way the gang had fled from the jail. They enquired from the people who lived in the nearby areas.

Now they drove through the road that ran near the jungle where Chakrapani and his gang had the hideout. There was a village a little far away. The police vehicle halted near the village. The SP sent his policemen to enquire in the village. Meanwhile he sat alone in the vehicle. A villager came running to him.

The man was *panting* deeply.

"Sir, I am sure that you are searching for the gang that had escaped from the jail." The man gasped.

"Yes, yes. Have you seen them?" asked Vikram with some hope.

"I saw a van coming near the jungle and disappeared suddenly!"

"Van disappearing? How is that possible?"

"I was sitting under that tree over there, cutting grass." He pointed to a tall tree, far away. "They couldn't see me. The van came at full speed and halted near the forest for a second and then it just vanished! After some time I went to the spot and found the tyre marks leading near to the forest and afterwards, I could find no trail at all!"

"I see, then they are hiding inside somewhere in the forest. If needed, can you help us in the future?"

"Sir, I am a simple villager having wife and children. I don't want to get into trouble. I am scared about the gang. If they come to know that I have helped you, they will kill me."

"Don't worry about your safety. I can assure you that no harm will come to you. I won't tell your name even to other policemen."

Vikram asked his contact number and the man after some *hesitation* gave his number.

Meanwhile SP Vikram saw some of the policemen coming to him.

"Okay, you may go now. If required, I will contact you." The villager went away.

The policemen reported to the SP that they could not get any evidence. SP Vikram asked the driver to take them to the spot where the gang had supposed to have vanished. He got down from the vehicle and examined the spot very thoroughly. Other policemen too followed him. They could see the tyre marks but surprisingly failed to see where the vehicle had disappeared.

The SP asked the policemen to check whether they could drive into the forest. The driver tried to take the van inside but it hit on the creepers. Suddenly one of the front tyres was flattened as it got punctured. They examined the ground and found that there were planks laid all around with sharp nails pointed upwards. It was clear that the nails were planted deliberately to prevent anyone from entering the forest. From that Vikram concluded that the gang had made a hideout somewhere inside the forest.

"It's not possible for us to drive inside the forest from this side," Vikram told the policemen. "The gang must have laid nails all around the forest and if it's so, we can't operate using our vehicles."

"Sir, I think then we should try aerial attack," one of the policemen suggested.

"I was planning the same thing. We can try using a helicopter. If the gang is hiding inside, they may try to shoot at the helicopter, but that mustn't stop us from trying."

"I feel that we must not try aerial attack immediately because the gang may be well prepared to *bounce* back on us. We must go for a surprise attack when they least expect it," another policeman said.

"Okay, we shall wait for some time. Now that a tyre

is punctured, is there a spare - tyre to replace the punctured one?" Vikram enquired.

"Fortunately, yes sir," the driver said.

"Thank god for that." Vikram heaved a sigh. "In this remote village we may hardly find a work shop where they repair punctured tyres."

The punctured tyre was replaced and soon they drove back to the station. Vikram again thought about Super Kid and wondered why he did not appear.

Soon arrangements were made for an aerial attack next week.

Meanwhile Chakrapani was informed about the *futile* attempt made by the police to enter the forest. Chakrapani and his gang watched it on the CCTV screen. Chakrapani had hijacked a technician, named Damodar, to install hidden cameras and CCTV around the forest. Damodar was forced to undertake the job as he had no other option. Once the work was done, luckily his life was spared as his help might be required in the future. He was locked up in a cell.

Now that the gangsters came to know about the police attack, they intensified their security arrangements to prevent any more attacks. The villager, who had reported about the disappearance of the van, was not captured on the CCTV camera as that area was not under its *surveillance*.

SP Vikram thought about another plan, an attempt to get into the jungle using a tank. He got it arranged and under him a team of policemen followed the tank.

As the tank was driven into the forest, the fencing of the forest tumbled down. A road was seen going into the forest. But suddenly arrows *whizzed* through the air towards the tank and one of them hit the driver on his chest. The man screamed piteously and fell forward.

"Lift the man from the tank and take him to safety. He is hit badly. Hurry up!" Vikram ordered.

Some of the policemen rushed to the tank cautiously and pulled the man out. They carried him into the Scorpio.

SP Vikram examined the man's pulse.

"Oh, my God! He's DEAD!!" Vikram said sadly. Everyone became disturbed and sad.

Immediately arrows came from everywhere and hit the Scorpio. A few policemen were standing near the tank.

"Get into the Scorpio, we must leave here immediately," Vikram cried. He didn't want to lose any more of his men again.

"Now we have only one option left, aerial attack," Vikram told as they were fleeing from the site.

Vikram briefed his superior officer about the operation and pleaded for more time to trace the criminals. The officer *complied* with his request.

After a few days, Vikram, along with a few policemen, flew in a helicopter and approached the forest. As they reached the forest, arrows and bullets hit on the helicopter.

"Fly higher. We must go back, it's risky to venture further," Vikram told his men. Soon they flew away to safety. Now he realized that the area was well protected by the gang and *trespassing* into the territory could be fatal.

"It appears impossible to *trespass* into Chakrapani's *impregnable* fortress!" One of the policemen said.

"No, I'm not ready to give up!" There was resolution in SP Vikram's words.

The SP informed the DGP about their adventure and asked his advice about another attack. He asked Vikram to halt the operation for the time being and wait for his further orders.

Vikram desperately wished for Super Kid's help, but in vain. Chakrapani and his gang had a merry laugh on the other side.

27

The Three secrets

Veeru Dada got a phone call from Stephen the next day. He told Veeru Dada, "Come to my office at three o'clock today and take the amount you wanted."

Veeru Dada was confused and wondered as why Stephen was offering him some money. But at the same time he was excited as he was going to get some amount. He had forgotten about the identity of Super Kid, though it was revealed to him by Durasar. All the four people, Veeru Dada, the two gangsters and Durasar, only knew the secret but Super Kid had deleted it from their minds!

Veeru Dada, this time *disguised* as a Pathan, reached Stephen's office on time. He just opened the door and entered the room.

Stephen looked up and seeing a Pathan entering his office without knocking, became angry.

"Hey, who are you?"

Veeru Dada just removed his beard and said smilingly: "Look here, sir!"

"Oh, it's you Veeru again. I couldn't recognize you even though I had asked you to meet me this time. You are extremely smart in the art of disguising!"

"One has to be smart enough if one wants to survive as a criminal!"

"Well said. Now tell me the secret. I can't wait any longer to hear it."

"Secret? What secret?"

"Are you out of your senses, man? You had rung me up yesterday saying that you were going to tell me three secrets, the whereabouts of Jim and two more something. How come you forgot about them?"

Veeru Dada *racked* his brain, but couldn't remember anything. After some time he told Stephen, "I haven't rung you up yesterday, you are mistaken."

"Then why did you come here today?"

"You told me that you want to give me some amount."

"What rubbish! I had already given you fifty thousand in advance for finding the whereabouts of Jim. Have you forgotten that too?"

"I haven't forgotten that. Still I am searching for him."

"Hurry up man. You have got many useless fellows in your gang, why don't you engage them with this mission?"

"I have the photograph of Jim that you had given me. With the help of it I'm sure to find the kid. But I haven't found him yet and I hadn't spoken with you yesterday."

"It's very confusing. You spoke with me yesterday and I wonder why you deny it today."

"That's what I too am worried"
"Go away. If you succeed to remember it, call me at once."

Veeru Dada left the office in utter confusion. While going towards his hide-out he looked around to check whether Super Kid was following him. He heaved a sigh of relief as there was no attack from Super Kid.

He changed his disguise and sat down in the hall. Shankar, a senior member from his gang, came to him and asked: "What shall we do with the kid lying in the room?"

"Kid, which kid?" Veeru Dada, who had totally forgotten about him, enquired surprisingly.

"Even I don't remember who has brought him here. But Pappu says that we, that's you, boss, Divakar and myself had brought him, but surprisingly none of us is aware of it! The child was unconscious."

"Is it so? It's very surprising. Even Stephen told me that I was supposed to tell him three secrets. I don't know any secret at all!" He paused for some time and then continued, "Anyway, let me see the kid. May be we can make use of him to steal things for us."

Sankar asked Pappu to bring the child in. Pappu went to the room and came running alone.

"Boss, he's not in the room!"

"What the hell are you telling? How come he's missing? How can a child run away from here? He may report about us. The police may find out our hide-out!"

Very much perturbed, Veeru Dada rang the bell and his gang came running.

"What were you doing, you lazy and good -for- nothing fellows? Couldn't you keep watch over a kid?" The Don was furious. "Come on, search everywhere, every nook and corner and I want him here AT ONCE."

"I had seen him just a few seconds ago," one of the gangsters said.

"Then, did he vanish into the thin air or did the earth swallow him up? Stop *blabbering* and go and find out him immediately."

The gang at once began their search everywhere but Jim was not seen anywhere. Finally it was concluded that he had run away.

There was much panic and Veeru Dada became mad with rage. He began to kick and slap his gang.

"None of you guys will get food for three days!" He yelled at the top of his voice.

x   x   x   x

Jim had woken up in the early morning. He looked around and took a few moments to recall what had happened. His kidnap drama flashed in his memory – a sudden blast followed by smoke around, and masked people carrying him. Next what he remembered was the face of Veeru Dada and his jeering, "Open your eyes, Jim, no, the great Super Kid! Now we know your identity and you are finished! Super Kid! Bah!! You and your baton! I'll flog you to death!" He recalled how he acted promptly by saying the words," may all those who know my identity forget it!"

Now he became worried about his family, his new parents, Victor and Stella, his own most dear little sister, Jane, and his two friends, Jerry and Marina.

Without losing any more time, using his divine power as Super Kid, he went around invisible and studied the location. Using his power as Super Kid, he made the gang to sleep for a longer time. He opened the door using his power and came out. He could find that the hide - out was in an old *dilapidated* building near the main road.

It was early dawn which was really enchanting and *invigorating*. The sun had not started peeping. There was only a dim light.

He ran to the main road and got into a rickshaw which brought him to his home after about two hour's ride.

As the rickshaw proceeded, the sun slowly emerged in the sky and began to spread its glorious light.

At that time Victor, Stella, Jerry and Marina were at home. Jerry and Marina were inside the room still crying and utterly desperate at the missing of their beloved Jim.

Jim rang the doorbell. Victor opened the door. Seeing

Jim he was overjoyed and shouted in excitement, "look, who is here! Our Jim has come back!!"

Others came running with *exhilaration.*

"Oh, where were you, dearest Jim?" Stella embraced him. Jane *hugged* him and started crying with joy. Jerry and Marina were also extremely happy.

"Give me my fare, please." The rickshaw walla shouted.

"Oh, yes. Let me send this man away," Victor said and went to the man and asked, "How much is the rickshaw fare?"

"Only three hundred and fifty rupees, sir."

"Three hundred and fifty?"

"Yes, sir. It took nearly two hours to reach here."

"No problem, man. Take five hundred instead, for bringing our beloved child here safe and sound."

"Thank you, sir. It's kind of you. How come, this young boy was alone in a faraway place?"

"Oh, that's a long story. You may go now. We are too eager to hear a number of things from him."

The rickshaw driver left, at once.

"Now tell us, Jim, what had happened. We are too impatient to hear it from you," said Victor.

"I was kidnapped by a gang. When I woke up in the early morning they were sleeping and I managed to come out stealthily, got into the rickshaw and reached here. Otherwise I don't know anything about the gang as I was unconscious because of the spray they had used."

"Okay. Let me report to the SP about Jim's return and I also will inform the principal as well."

Meanwhile, Jim's other self, Super Kid, reached the SP's office. The SP was seated in his office, glancing through the criminal record.

"Sir, I'm back," Super Kid told in a low voice.

"Oh, Super Kid, how happy I'm to meet you again. Actually I was desperately looking for you!"

"For some unexpected reasons I couldn't come to you when you were urgently in need of my help."

At the very moment there was a call from Victor. The SP attended the call.

"Sir, I made this call to tell you that Jim has come back."

"Oh, really? It's indeed a great news. Where was he?"

"Someone had kidnapped him, but he escaped very cleverly when they were asleep."

"I want to enquire a number of things from him. Let him relax today. Tomorrow is Saturday and he doesn't have school. Bring him here tomorrow, by twelve o'clock."

"Yes, sir. I'll do as you said."

The SP disconnected the phone, and then narrated to Super Kid his team's unsuccessful attempt to recapture Chakrapani and his gang.

"Don't worry sir. I'll go into Chakrapani's hideout in the jungle and find out the situation there. You are an honest police officer and I can assure you of my full support to nab the criminals. Adieu for the time being. I'll meet you soon, after exploring the Chakrapani's hide-out!"

Super Kid disappeared.

28

Super Kid surveys Chakrapani's hide-out

Chakrapani and his gang were making merry inside their hide-out. The gang had brought a dance group from outside, at gun point, and the criminals were enjoying the dance. They were sure that the SP and his team wouldn't be able to find out them.

Super Kid went around and studied the hide-out, invisible to the gang.

He found Sharma, the guard, who had helped Chakrapani to escape. Chakrapani had promised to reward him but the cunning criminal had made Sharma a prisoner in his hide-out. Sharma looked quite weak and utterly desperate.

In another room Super Kid saw, Damodar, the software technician, who was kidnapped by Chakrapani to install CCTV cameras in the forest. He was a young man in his early twenties, who had cherished sweet dreams for a bright future. Super Kid saw him sitting near a window in utter despair.

Now Super Kid appeared to Sharma, who was taken aback to find such a strange figure.

"You may not have heard about me. I am known as Super Kid and I'm here to help you to be out of here. You had committed an extremely serious crime, helping a notorious Don and his gang to escape from the prison. I hope that by now you have realized the gravity of your crime."

"Am I seeing a dream? I can't believe what I see and hear." Sharma was still not able to believe.

"I know that it's not easy to believe me, because it's something very unexpected and strange. I know all about you and your family. Your son, Ravi, is studying in the seventh class, in the Green Valley English medium school. You family is leading a miserable life without knowing about your whereabouts. They are not even sure whether you are alive or not."

"I'm desperate here thinking about them and I spend my life in fear and uncertainty. Any time the Don may kill me!" Sharma shivered at the thought."Now I realize the seriousness of my crime and I am ready to confess it and am ready to accept any punishment. My only worry is about my family." There were tears in his eyes, which gleamed in the dim light.

"I'll help you to be out of here, but then you need to surrender to the law which will take its own course."

"I promise you that definitely I'll surrender to the law. But how can you, a mere kid, help me to escape from this notorious and powerful Don? His gang is everywhere in this jungle, keeping watch twenty four hours."

"Believe in God's mercy and providence, and miracle will happen."

"How much I long to meet my family, my dear wife and our only son, Ravi! I am ready for anything if I escape from these dreaded criminals."

Super Kid held his hand and brought him to the door which was locked from outside. As they approached the door, it opened suddenly and to the great surprise of Sharma he found all the gang fallen unconscious. There was unusual stillness as in a *graveyard*.

"The doors just open automatically, he has supernatural powers!" Sharma told to himself. "How strange, not a single criminal is awake!"

"Now, you stay here. Be confident. No harm will come to you. I want to release one more person, a software engineer, who is imprisoned in another room."

Super Kid next released Damodar, the software engineer, who was also completely astounded and couldn't believe his eyes.

Super Kid woke up a driver and using his power, made him to drive them out of the jungle safely. The driver didn't utter a word; he was just following the instruction given by Super Kid, as if under a spell.

Finally they came out of the jungle and reached their destination. The driver drove back and reached the hide-out.

There was great joy and relief in the families of Sharma and Damodar.

Next Super Kid appeared in front of the SP and informed him the details about the hide-out of Chakrapani. He also briefed him how he had rescued Sharma and Damodar.

"So Sharma was under the custody of Chakrapani. I am happy to learn that he has surrendered to the court," Vikram told Super Kid. "When Chakrapani and his notorious gang wake up, they will be shocked and puzzled by the missing of their 'prisoners'."

"I have found a secret tunnel between two rocks which is used by the gang to pass through. You can take the police force through this secret path. You all have to crawl as the tunnel is very low in height. At the end of the tunnel you will find the hide – out of the gang. Nobody is keeping watch at this place. After reaching the hide – out, you will be able to capture them. I will be following you and only you will be able to see me."

"I am indebted to you Super Kid, for all your help."

"It's all God's doing. You needn't acknowledge my share in this operation anywhere. Only thank God for the success in nabbing the criminals."

The police force went through the jungle road and reached the hide-out of Chakrapani. Chakrapani and his gang were surprised seeing the force, tried to resist, but the force pounced upon them like a lion on its prey and they were caught red handed. They found a large stock of ammunition, guns, bombs, drugs, bows and arrows. They were in utter confusion, despair and shock. The police also observed a number of gangsters hiding on the trees with lethal weapons to keep watch. The police killed most of them and a few were arrested and taken along.

The recapture of the notorious gang was a *shot in the arm* for the police force, under SP Vikram. The DGP congratulated Vikram and the team for their success.

The news of the capture of Chakrapani gladdened Veeru Dada and his gang as well.

29

Veeru Dada's encounter with Stephen

Now that Chakrapani and his gang were in the jail, Veeru Dada thought to expand his 'business' to further heights. He wanted money for the same, that too fast money, without much effort. He didn't have to think much, just picked up his mobile and rang up to Stephen.

"Yes, Veeru, tell me what do you want now?" Stephen enquired trying to hide his irritation.

Stephen had lost his impression of Veeru Dada as he had not succeeded to find out Jim. Besides, he acted in a funny manner promising to tell three secrets and later on completely forgotten about them! Thereafter Stephen decided to avoid him as far as possible.

"I need some amount, urgently."

"How dare you ask me? Am I your banker? If you need money, you must think about ways to raise it. After all you are a Don, should I advise you how to make money?"

"Why boss, you sound a bit irritated. Don't forget the relation we have maintained so far."

"What kind of relation, man. Are you my brother or friend?"

"Yes, in a way, we are brothers in crime!" Veeru chuckled.

"Don't fool around with me, I have no time for trifles. Come to the point. How much is your requirement?"

"Not much, just ten lakhs. I know it's not a big amount for you!"

"How dare you speak to me like that? I needed your help in the past and I've paid you for the same. Last time I've given you fifty thousand in advance to find out the whereabouts of Jim. You haven't succeeded yet. If you are not capable, return the amount. I will look for somebody else. I think time has come for us to separate!"

"Hello, boss, speak sense. You can't get rid of me, thus. I know some of your secrets, if I disclose them to the police, just guess what's going to happen to you. You will be behind the bars for the rest of your life."

"I have told you several times not to talk such things over the phone. Come here; let us talk about across the table."

"No, problem, boss. I'll be there after an hour. Listen boss, one more thing. A breaking news for you – I will be disclosing to you a secret today definitely, which will make you sweat like anything and you will offer me anything I ask you thereafter. So don't forget about my requirement, just keep it ready."

"Like last time's promise!" Stephen said to himself.

Stephen cut the call from the other side. He was much *perturbed*, threw his mobile on the table and lost in thought. He realized that Veeru was going to be a nuisance, a thorn to be pulled out and thrown away!

"What could be that great secret? *Rubbish*. The guy has lost his senses." Stephen was much tensed and lost in thought.

As it was decided, Veeru Dada reached Stephen's office disguised as a Sardarji. This time Stephen guessed that it was Veeru Dada.

Veeru Dada pulled a chair and sat down. Stephen was not all pleased to meet him.

"Now come to the point, straight away. Hereafter never talk over the phone anything personal."

"No problem. Make me happy occasionally and your secret will be safe with me. But if you try to be over smart, you will land in trouble."

"Stop that threatening tone. If ever I land in the jail, you too will be with me. Just mind it."

"If you are caught, you will lose all the wealth you are enjoying now, because you have got it by being a *fraud*. You will become a BIG ZERO! If ever I land behind bars, I will be back after some time as I have my gang to help me out."

"Now let's talk to the point. What do you want the money for?"

"That's personal. You needn't know it."

"What do you expect from me, just pay ten lakhs to a stupid Don? Don't expect a single paisa from me hereafter. Come, what may."

"Okay, fine. I had expected that any time you may act over smart. Look at this video which I had shot yesterday just to show you. Let me watch and enjoy the expression on your face! "

Veeru Dada took out his mobile, started a video and gave it to Stephen.

"Look at the bearded man, you will know him very well, the one who can make you a ZERO once again!"

After watching the video clip, Stephen was frozen in his seat and looked pale! After some time he yelled desperately: "YOU CHEAT!!"

"This man is under my custody and if I produce him, you are going to be a zero, a big zero. Ha! Ha! Ha!!" Veeru Dada chuckled viciously and Stephen sweated profusely though the room had air cooler.

Jim's other self, Super Kid, had followed Veeru Dada. He remained invisible to them and listened to their conversation. He also looked at the video just out of curiosity but after seeing the person in it, he too stood frozen, with a mixed expression of happiness, excitement and shock!

A dead man becomes alive!

"My dearest dad is alive!" Jim was thrilled and overjoyed. He felt like thanking Veeru Dada for keeping his father alive.

"Why did you do this to me, man?" Stephen screamed *pathetically*. "Why did you not kill Vincent sir? Now where have you kept him, hidden?"

"Hello, boss! I'm made of a different stuff, a real tough stuff indeed. I am a very shrewd criminal, a criminal to the core. Now don't think that I'm a fool to tell you where I've kept him. If you come to know, either you will finish Vincent sir, the real owner of this company, or get him killed with the help of somebody else and put the blame on me."

"But....but you had shown me a video clip of the accident scene, as a proof. In the video I could see Vincent Sir seated in his car and you were pushing the vehicle with a truck. Finally the car rolled down deep into the valley and caught fire."

"Yes, I did show you the video which was real. The

video was shot by my friend. But the man you saw in the video was ...." Veeru just stopped to watch the plight of Stephen – like a cat plays with a mouse before killing it!

"Please.....who was the man?"

"Unfortunately for you, boss, it was a dummy of Vincent sir! Ha! Ha! Ha!"

"But why did you not kill him?"

"It was because...." He paused again in order to create tension for Stephen. He continued after some time, "I suspected rightly that any time you may try to avoid me; that you may sometime act too smart. I am smart, damn smart, and can't stand smarter people, you see."

He looked at Stephen and enjoyed the disappointment and fear writ on his face.

"Now, my demand is not a meager ten lakh, but FIFTY – FIFTY!"

"What the hell is this damn fifty-fifty?" Stephen banged in his table and asked. He was getting more and more irritated and desperate.

"Oh, that's a simple calculation – So far you were enjoying the wealth of Vincent sir. Hereafter we'll have equal share, that's fifty-fifty. If it's acceptable to you, say 'yes', just now. Vincent Sir will remain in my custody safely as long as I want to keep him. Once I get what I want, I'll kill him myself. If your reply is 'no', I hope you won't be so foolish to say 'no', I will produce him in the court. And then the court procedure, trial, a lot of botheration and finally you will lose all the wealth that you had raised through cheating and forgery, then your imprisonment, the judgment.... You could be ordered to be hung till death!!"

When Super Kid heard his harsh words, he lost the appreciation he had cherished before for keeping his dad alive. "He is a criminal to the core who doesn't deserve any consideration," Super Kid told to himself.

Veeru Dada paused again and then continued, "Once you lose your wealth, your wife will desert you again, that's certain. As far as your son, John, is concerned, he will surely turn into a bigger criminal than you are. You can be proud of him! Ha! Ha!"

"You, rascal, good for nothing fellow, the cheat, you are crossing the limit."

"Your worry won't last longer because you are sure to be hanged for killing Sir's wife." Veeru enjoyed jeering at Stephen and creating terror in him.

Stephen was almost mad with rage. Stephen drew his drawer, grabbed his gun and pointed it at Veeru. "Now you are finished Veeru! See, who is going to die first."

He was about to pull the trigger, but Veeru acted promptly. He fell sidewise and in a lightning speed caught hold off Stephen's leg and pulled him vigorously and the latter fell down with a thud sound. Veeru *snatched* the gun from his hand and pointed it at Stephen.

An uncomfortable *premonition* of fear pervaded the senses of Stephen.

"I had already told you not to act too smart. Now taste a shot from your own gun. To the police, it will look like you have committed suicide! Do you want to say a prayer? It's customary to ask for the last wish. I'll give you time to think."

Super Kid watched them and knew what was going to happen. So he didn't interfere. He stood an invisible *mute spectator*.

Stephen was speechless. There was terror in his eyes and the Don enjoyed watching it.

"All the wealth and comfort that I have been enjoying….. What's going to happen to me and to my wealth?" Stephen told in his mind desperately. "Am I going to lose the wealth I have amassed so far? How can I save myself?"

Veeru Dada watched the miserable expression on Stephen's face, which had become pale with terror and anxiety. After some time the Don asked banteringly, "Now are you ready to embrace death?"

Stephen sat speechless and motionless. He was still without any *compunction* for his past evil ways but was thinking deeply as how to overpower the Don.

"Okay, now I end our 'rat and mouse game' to give relief from your agony. Tell me finally; are you ready to share fifty percentage of your wealth?" The Don enquired still pointing the gun at him.

"First keep the gun aside. Let me speak. I…..eh am ready for it!" Stephen said still quite *reluctantly*.

"Okay, so the deal is going to be made." The Don smiled and kept the gun in his pocket.

"Give me my gun, please."

"I'm not an idiot. Once you get your gun back, you are surely going to shoot me dead, aren't you? Should I give you a chance to get killed, like a fool?" asked Veeru Dada sardonically.

"Look, Veeru. Now we have made a deal and let's be friends or rather continue as 'brothers in crime'!"

"I have no trust in you. You have cheated a man who had given you a job and shelter. You conspired to get him killed. How can I trust you? Besides, you wanted to get rid of me. Then how can I believe your words?"

"Then how are we going to settle the matter between us?"

"First transfer fifty percentage of the wealth that you are enjoying now, to my account. Here is my account number."

The Don quickly wrote his account number and other details on a piece of paper and passed it to Stephen.

"Now I'm taking your leave. Don't act over smart by calling your gang to finish me. My men are alert and they won't spare you. So be wise and be a good boy! Your gun will be safe with me. I consider it as a gift from your side. Bye, take care!!" His sarcastic tone further irritated Stephen but he controlled his temper as there was no other option.

Veeru Dada left the office with a sense of *accomplishment*. "Now I'll be more powerful and richer than Chakrapani. You are a very clever fellow, Veeru Dada, the great Don!" The Don said to himself as he moved towards his Honda city.

Super Kid now followed Veeru Dada. His aim was to find out his beloved dad.

31

The mystery of the 'special prisoner'

The jubilant Veeru Dada went to his car, opened it slowly, got into the driver's seat, closed the door, locked it, started the engine, cranked the AC and off he went to his destination. Super Kid sat on the seat next to him, invisible. The Don drove for some time and was excited thinking about his future.

"Hello, Veeru!" Super Kid called him from the next seat.

The Don screamed in terror, seeing no one but at the same time hearing a voice from the next seat.

"WHO……..who are you? " He trembled like a leaf. "Where ……..are you? I …….I can't see you."

"You are a very bold man. Why are you shivering?" asked Super Kid.

"Show yourself. Are you that damn Super Kid? Your voice is familiar."

"You are right. Look, I'm sitting next to you." Super Kid now made himself visible to the Don.

"You, Super Kid again!" He *shrieked* with a mixture of anger and fear. He involuntarily pressed his leg on the brake and brought the car to a shuddering stop.

"Yes, and I'm sure you are not very pleased to meet me again." Super Kid smiled.

"First get out of my car. I don't want to go through that humiliating ordeal again. I'll never forget your baton."

"Only criminals are scared of me and try to avoid me. The needy ones wait eagerly for my help."

"I'm not at all interested to have a conversation with you. Let me live in peace."

"You criminals can never live in peace, because you are under the power of the devil and always think of doing harm to others. Your conscience always pricks you. Only those who have God's presence in them, can experience real peace."

"I don't understand such language. I'm happy with what I'm doing. Now please……PLEASE leave me."

"Tell me where you have kept Jim's dad. Show him and I'll leave you for the time being."

"I don't know what you are speaking. Which Jim, which dad?"

The Don got a severe shock. Until now he thought that he, Pappu, his servant, and now Stephen knew that

Vincent sir was alive! An uncomfortable premonition of fear pervaded his senses.

"I know all about you, and about Jim's dad. Stephen had entrusted you the task of killing Jim's dad, but you had very cleverly kept him alive in your custody with the evil intention – to demand money from Stephen, in short to black mail him!"

"How the hell do you know all these?" asked Veeru Dada *petulantly*.

"Don't you know that I'm Super Kid having divine powers? Take me to Vincent sir."

"NO!" Veeru Dada screamed with growing rage. He *gnashed* his teeth.

"You, criminal won't understand mild language. Then take this dose of heat *therapy*!"

Immediately the Don felt that his seat was slowly becoming hot and then gradually the heat kept on increasing. He saw steam spreading around him! At once he leaped from his seat with a scream.

"Hey stop! I'm burning!!"

Now the inside of the car turned into a furnace. He bent down and looked out for help, but surprisingly nobody was around. He desperately tried to open the door, but it didn't yield.

"Nobody will come for your help. You will burn yourself inside your car. If you want me to stop the heat from hurting you, take me to Vincent sir."

"Please......stop it. I'll do anything you say!" the Don groaned helplessly.

"Okay, then start your car and let's go!"

While driving, the Don was desperate. He racked his brain for an idea to get rid of the Kid. He applied the brake suddenly and the car stopped with a screeching sound. He opened the door on the left side of the car and tried to push Super Kid out. But as he stretched his hand to push the boy, his hand became *numb*. He realized that his left hand was frozen.

He screamed:"Ouch! I can't move my hand!!"

"You are a wicked man, who can never be trusted! You will try anything for your safety and monetary gain! Now drive with one hand and don't think any more evil tricks !"

"Please, save my hand. I won't do anything more to offend you."

"If you are really sorry for your doing, you are getting your hand back."

As his hand became normal, the Don heaved a sigh of relief. Thereafter he didn't dare any more tricks.

Finally they reached his hide-out. The Don alighted from the car and when looked at the other seat, lo! Super Kid was not there. "Ah! That damn kid has finally gone to hell! Super Kid, shit!! If I get his baton, I'll burn it in the fire!"

He called for his servant, "Pappu, how's our special prisoner? Have you given him something to eat?"

Veeru Dada enquired.

"Yes, master. I've given something for him just to survive."

"Yes, that's all. But he must just survive. Don't tell anybody where we have kept him," the Don warned. "I'm going to check his condition, make sure that no one follows me."

"Yes, master. I'll be waiting here, you can see him."

Super Kid followed the Don, invisible.

The Don went through a corridor, entered a room, opened it with a key that was kept in his pocket, looked around to check whether anyone was around and bolted the door from inside. Next he pushed aside a box kept on the corner of the room and under it, a lever was seen. Using the lever, he lifted a heavy metal lid. Steps were seen leading to an underground room. The Don carefully went down though the steps and finally reached the ground where sat Vincent sir, Jim's father, on the floor.

Hearing the sound of steps, the man raised his head, opened his eyes and gazed at the Don with a mixed expression of pleading, anger, uncertainty and fear.

Super Kid now saw his father in a pitiable state. He was extremely happy to see his father but at the same time felt miserable seeing the sad plight of his beloved dad.

"Oh, my dad, my dearest dad, how can I see you suffering so much!" Jim groaned and tears welled up in his eyes.

Vincent sir looked very pathetic. He was quite weak

and lean. His hair and beard had grown very long which made him looking older than he was. His eyes had sunk. In the place of a handsome man, now there was a man with pathetic features, looking like a beggar! There was a foul smell in the room.

"Why have you come here again? Why don't you kill me and end this miserable life?" Vincent sir asked in a pitiful tone. It was the voice of one who had lost all hope. "Will I be able to meet my family any time?"

"You are a 'golden goose' for me. That's why I don't want to kill you immediately. But once I achieve my goal, I don't mind ending your suffering. Now I have come to verify that you are not dead."

Hearing the harsh words, Jim got wild and gave the Don a push and the latter fell face down.

"Hey, who pushed me, I'll finish that fellow." He looked around and found none. "That damn kid must be here somewhere."

He struggled to his feet and began to beat around like a mad man. Vincent sir watched him and wondered whether the criminal had gone mad. Finally exhausted by the futile exercise, the Don sat down. Now Super Kid made him unconscious, using his power.

Vincent sir wondered what happened to him. Jim appeared before his dad as Super Kid. Vincent sir was shocked seeing an unusual figure appearing suddenly from nowhere.

"Hey, ...who ....are you? How did you appear suddenly?"

Jim changed his voice so as to avoid his dad recognizing him and said, "I'm known as Super Kid. I am given divine power to help the needy and punish the guilty. I am a friend of God-fearing people, but a terror to the criminals."

"I..........I don't feel like believing it. It's very strange, very unusual, and something incredible. Can you help me to be out of here? How I long to meet my family! Stephen, whom I had helped, made my life miserable!"

"I know all about you. Please have faith in God's providence. God has seen your misery and has heard your prayers. Now I've made this criminal unconscious and I'm going to take you out from here."

So saying, Jim held his dad's hand and led him through the steps. Jim felt extremely happy in holding his father's hands, but couldn't reveal his identity as angel Shalom had forbidden him to do so. Vincent sir felt a special affection towards Super Kid, like a father's fondness towards his son.

Finally they came to the room, Super Kid bolted the door leading to the underground and came out. Slowly they went through the corridors and finally were out of the hide-out! Surprisingly nobody was found around there! To Vincent sir everything was like a dream, a sweet dream!

They got into a rickshaw and reached Victor's house. Vincent sir got out of the rickshaw and looking at the house, he stood wondering whose house it was. Super Kid rang the doorbell, Victor opened the door and seeing Super Kid and Vincent sir, he stood *flabbergasted!*

32

A family reunion

"Aren't you Vincent, my dearest friend?" With *ecstasy*, Victor ran to him and hugged Vincent sir.

"Victor, my best friend, how happy I'm to meet you!" Vincent sir couldn't believe his eyes.

"You look quite miserable. What has happened to you, friend? We were the best friends in the school and Junior College, but afterwards, we lost touch with each other," Victor told with a lot of concern.

"What a pleasant surprise, to meet you, Victor, my bosom friend. I always longed to meet you, desperately, but I had no information about your whereabouts. I had changed my Sim card and thus lost your contact number. Here is Super Kid. It's because of him I am alive and standing before you! I can never thank him adequately," said Vincent sir.

"It's all God's doing! I knew about your friendship and that's why I bought you here," Super Kid smiled.

"I want to hear in detail all about you, your family and of course, about this wonder -kid. I am thrilled to meet him. I had heard about him from my children but never had an opportunity to see him. Someone had stolen my mobile and consequently I had lost all my contact numbers. What are you doing, Vincent? I'm sure you are well placed in your life, because you were the brightest student in our class, an all-rounder," Victor was eager to know about his friend.

They recalled the best days of their life, always together, studying, going for movies, picnics, outing, parties etc. Those were the most enjoyable and memorable days.

"I had a small company called 'Trinity Enterprises', but ....it's a long story. I'll tell you about it later on. Tell me about yourself. While you studied for LLB, I pursued MBA. After the completion of the courses, unfortunately, we couldn't get in touch." Vincent felt an agonizing pain when he thought about his family and the company.

"You said you had a small company! You are very humble, my friend. I had, of course, heard about your flourishing and esteemed company, but was not aware that you are the owner. Now, as far as I am concerned, I am a practicing lawyer."

"I'm sure you must be faring exceptionally well as an advocate because you were very brilliant. You must be a very famous advocate, but I wonder why I haven't heard your name."

"I am known as advocate Immanuel, not Victor," Victor smiled.

"The famous advocate Immanuel! My God, you are the one? Yes, it has to be my friend. You had won many sensational cases. You were in the news, but your photo was missing in the cover up."

"I didn't want my photo to be published."

Just then Stella came out and surprised to find her husband talking with a miserably looking stranger. He pointed out to her and said, "By the by, meet my other half - Stella." He turned to his wife and introduced his friend, "He is my best friend, Vincent, about whom I've told you several times."

Stella was very happy to hear it. She smiled warmly and said, "Welcome to our home. Not a day passed without my husband talking about you! Who is this child?"

"He is the famous hero, the one and the only SUPER KID!!"

Stella was thrilled to hear it and embraced the child affectionately.

"What a pleasant surprise! We are blessed and lucky to have both of you. Please take your seats and relax. Let me bring a drink." Stella turned to go in.

"Don't prepare anything for me. I need to go now," said Super Kid.

"Oh, don't go now." Vincent sir said quite sadly. "I couldn't thank you sufficiently for what you have done. Of course, no words can adequately express my gratitude."

"You needn't thank me. Be grateful to God because it's His doing, I was only an instrument in carrying out his Divine plan."

"Our children would've been excited to meet you," said Stella a bit disappointed.

"I'll be meeting them, later on. Now I have an urgent work to carry out. Adieu, for the time being."

"If it's so urgent, we have nothing more to tell you," said Victor.

Super Kid vanished and all stood speechless.

"Meet my children. We have four children. Jerry and Marina are our biological children and we have another two whom we have adopted. They are also now our OWN children," Victor smiled.

First Jerry and Marina appeared and Victor introduced them. Then Jim and Jane came out.

Seeing Jim and Jane, Vincent sir stood paralyzed with ecstasy and excitement, "Oh My God, my dearest children Jim and Jane!" The children ran to their father with excitement and joy. Vincent sir embraced them most *affectionately*.

"What? Are they your children?" asked Victor equally excited.

"What a coincidence, so incredible!" said Stella, amazed by the series of surprises.

"Where were you daddy, we missed you so badly," Jane cried with a mixed feeling of joy and sorrow.

"How much we longed to meet you, dearest daddy!" Jim also couldn't control his tears.

"If only your mummy also were to be here!" Tears

rolled down from Vincent's eyes. Veeru Dada had already informed him that Stephen had killed her. "We miss her, really miss her," Jim said and wept.

"Our dearest mom.....," Jane also wept.

"It's not the time for weeping. At least, thank God for uniting all of you!" Victor consoled them. "What a coincidence, but it's *awesome!*"

"It's all so amazing! We have watched such cases only on the screen!!" Stella said.

"Vincent, please have a bath." He turned to his wife and said," Stella, prepare tea and snacks. We shall hear more about Vincent and his experience, later on." Victor led his friend to the bath room.

Vincent sir still couldn't believe that he was finally free and all the more that he could meet his children again. He moved about as if in a dream.

Having completed the bath and breakfast, the two friends shared their experience after their college life – their career, marriage, family and so on. So also Vincent and his children shared their experience. Jim told his father how he had left home and reached Victor's house but kept the Super Kid episode still confidential.

"I have heard about Trinity enterprises. I didn't know that my best friend was the owner of such a flourishing company. I'll plead your case. I am sure you will get justice," Victor assured his friend.

"I have full faith in your *credibility*. I will surely want to meet the duo, Stephen and his wife! I hope Sam, our faithful driver is still safe," Vincent heaved a sigh of relief.

"He is still safe. He had called me a few days back," Jim told his dad.

"Oh, that's great news, indeed, I thank God!" said Vincent sir.

"We heard today a number of happy things. But............," Stella stopped abruptly.

"What's the matter? You look worried," asked Victor concerned.

"How can we think about parting with our dearest Jim and Jane?" There were tears in Stella's eyes. She wiped them suddenly with her hands.

"Even I thought about it and of course I'm also equally sad about it, but we can't keep them away from their father," Victor also expressed his concern.

"No, we won't allow them to go from here," Jerry said.

"Can't they continue living here with us?" Marina asked innocently.

"No dear, they will come with me to our home. But it will take some time. First we have to chase the criminals from our home, and keep them in the jail. Then only we can move in," said Vincent sir.

"Yes, the law will take its own course. The legal procedure will require time," Victor said. "All of us will surely miss Jim and Jane. They are so dear to us.

We never expected a time will come when we will be forced to part with them. Vincent, you will stay with us until the criminals are put behind the bars."

"Of course, thank you for your concern and taking care of our children."

"No formalities between us, Vincent."

"Okay, dear. My children will join me, but still we can all surely meet often," Vincent sir consoled them.

Vincent sir had his hair cut and shaving and once again looked almost as smart as before.

Next day, he decided to meet his arch enemy - Stephen, in his office. When he expressed his desire, Victor was apprehensive about his friend's safety. He wanted to accompany him but Vincent sir insisted that he wanted to go alone, disguised and told him about his plan. Finally Victor had to give in, though most unwillingly. "Suppose you smell anything fishy, I mean any danger, do call me. I'll come there with a police force."Vincent sir agreed and proceeded to his company in Victor's car.

33

Stephen's encounter with the 'stranger'

Vincent sir now reached his office, which was occupied by the wicked Stephen. He knocked at the door and just got inside. Stephen was seated on his chair and was checking some files on his computer.

He was surprised to see a Sardarji entering the office, that too without waiting for his permission. He was sure that it was none other than Veeru Dada in disguise.

"You, Veeru, have come here once again! I had told you that I'll be transferring half of my wealth into your account as you have demanded. But give me some time. Have you come to demand it now, or have you got some other crooked ideas to extract money from me?"

Hearing his words, Vincent sir became furious but controlled his temper.

"Why are you silent, you *wretched* Don?" Stephen was getting angry as the 'Sardarji' kept quiet. "Speak out or I'll blow your brains out!"

"Do you think that you can occupy this office for ever which had belonged to Vincent, the true owner?" Vincent sir asked.

"Your size is almost the same, but your voice is different. Aren't you Veeru Dada?" Stephen asked.

"Actually I've got a bad throat, that's why my voice sounds different," Vincent added promptly.

"I see, otherwise who will dare to enter here without permission?"

"Now suppose I produce Vincent, what will you do?"

"I'll blast his brain! I will not depend on you anymore because you have proved yourself a cheat."

"Aren't you a bigger cheat, enjoying another's hard earned money by getting the man killed, who had given you a job in his own company?"

"I'm destined to be a rich man. See, using my brain, how I have become the owner of a flourishing company. It's told, 'behind every great fortune, there is a crime', that's it. Now tell me, what's the purpose of your visit?"

"Nothing, just wanted to remind you about my fifty percent share! I want to go around and see your company, is it okay?"

"Why do you want to see my company? You have never expressed such a desire so far," Stephen again suspected whether it was Veeru Dada or someone else in disguise.

"Could it be a secret police to gather information and proof?" his suspicion grew stronger.

Stephen got up from his seat and walked towards Vincent sir. He asked him," Remove your turban and beard, let me see you, Veeru, I mean the real Veeru without this funny outfit."

Vincent sir got up, smelt danger. At the same time Super Kid whispered in his ears," Don't worry, sir, I'm here with you. No harm will come to you!"

Vincent sir felt extremely happy and relieved.

Stephen forcefully pulled Vincent Sir's turban and beard. Stephen stood frozen and his face turned pale as if he had seen a ghost!

"I'm a stranger!" Vincent sir said without any fear, because Super Kid was there with him.

"Vincent ......sir!" Stephen stammered and stood frozen.

"Yes, I am that same Vincent, your boss! You, ungrateful devilish fellow, conspired to get me killed by Veeru Dada! But God decided to spare me. So I'm here before you in flesh and blood!! I had failed to understand that I was feeding milk to a poisonous snake!"

Stephen caught hold of Vincent sir's neck and tried to *strangle* him.

"Yes, I wanted to kill you myself, but didn't want the police to suspect me. So I had entrusted the work to Veeru, who turned out to be a cheat. You had suspended me from the job but now I became the owner. That's the turn of fortune. Now you're finished man!"

Vincent released himself from Stephen's hold and gave him a mighty slap which made the wicked man swirl round and fall face downwards. He struggled to get up, but Vincent sir leaped on him and showered a number of punching with his fist. Stephen started bleeding profusely.

Stephen wiped the blood with his hand, then using all his strength threw Vincent sir away, got up, grabbed a gun and pointed it at him.

"Do you know what happened to your wife, Annie madam? I killed her MYSELF by creating a road accident. Now it's your turn. Ha! Ha! Ha!" The villain laughed again in a devilish manner.

Stephen was about to pull the trigger but suddenly the gun became boiling hot and it burnt his palm. He instantly threw it away. It fell near Vincent sir with a thud sound.

Super Kid sent his baton which began to beat the criminal black and blue. He writhed in pain and yelled, "Hey, stop, STOP!"

Somehow he managed to grab his gun and aimed it at Vincent sir. At the same moment the door of the office was flung open and SP Vikram and his policemen rushed in.

"FREEZE, Stephen!"

SP Vikram shouted and took the gun from him, covered it with a kerchief and handed it over to a policeman.

The SP continued, "We have sufficient evidence to prove that you have killed Mrs. Annie Vincent by creating a road accident. Veeru Dada has confessed his own guilt and at the same time has reported your share in all the crimes. Your game is over now, Stephen, the great criminal! Your stay in the cozy bungalow is over. It will remain *etched* in your memory as a sweet phase of your life. Hereafter you may count your remaining days in the stinking jail!"

SP Vikram caught his collar and pushed him to his policemen and yelled, "TAKE HIM!" The policemen dragged him to the police vehicle.

34

SP Vikram captures a dreaded Don

Super Kid appeared in front of SP Vikram. The police officer was in his house and was getting ready to go to the police station. He was extremely happy to meet Super Kid again who had helped him several times to bust the criminals.

"I'm very happy to meet you again. Actually I had just now thought about you and you are here in front of me," the police officer didn't *suppress* his joy.

"Chakrapani and his gang are in the jail, finally. Stephen is also in police custody. Now another Don, Veeru Dada, and his gang are very active in criminal activities," Super Kid said.

"Yes, I know. Thanks to your help, his two dreaded aids, Virendra and Vittal, are behind the bars. We are looking for Veeru Dada, but we haven't got any clue about his hide-out."

"I have found out his hide-out. I have already saved Vincent 'uncle' (Jim felt *awkward* again to speak about his own dad as uncle) from the '*custody*' of this criminal."

Jim explained to the SP about his adventurous operation.

"Vincent uncle is the real owner of the 'Trinity Enterprises', but his own accountant, Stephen uncle, another criminal, had engaged Veeru Dada to kill him in an accident. But the cunning Veeru Dada kept Vincent sir in his custody and pretended that he had killed him."

"What was his motive, certainly not a noble one?"

"He wanted to demand money from Stephen uncle by threatening to produce Vincent sir."

"I see. There are many criminal cases against Veeru and his gang. Once Chakrapani is put in the jail, Veeru will be emerging more powerful and will pose as a threat to the security of the common people."

"Sir, please come with me with your police force. I will take you to his hide-out. Only you will be able to see me. I've made the Don, Veeru Dada, unconscious and he is lying in an underground room, where he had hidden Vincent sir. I have made his gang to fall under a spell and you will be able to arrest them."

The SP rang up to the police station and asked the police force to be ready for an operation. Then the SP put on his uniform. The children had already gone to the school and his wife was getting ready to go to her office.

"Today you seem to be quite happy and relieved, what's the matter?"

"I had told you about another Don and his gang. Our next task is to capture them. I've got a clue about his hide-out. We are going for the operation, to put this gang also behind the bars."

"Oh, that's great news indeed. Please be very careful. The gang must be very dangerous."

"Don't worry, darling. You can go to your office, tension free. After our success, I'll let you know."

"I'll be praying for your safety and success and will be waiting to hear the good news."

"Okay, bye, dear."

The SP and Super Kid proceeded to the police station.

The police force along with the SP proceeded to the hide-out of Veeru Dada. Super Kid moved in front of the Swift in which SP Vikram and some senior police were travelling.

After about travelling for an hour, they reached the hide out. Veeru Dada and his gang were taken aback seeing the police force in their hide-out.

Super Kid led SP Vikram to the underground room where he saw Veeru Dada moving about in the room very much disturbed and in fury. Seeing the police officer and Super Kid he was shocked and gnashed his teeth in rage.

"You, Super Kid, made me unconscious and took away my prisoner! You made me spend hours in this filthy, stinking room! I won't spare you!!" Saying some abusing words, he charged at Super Kid.

SP Vikram slapped the criminal so strongly that Veeru Dada lost his balance and fell down.

"I was looking for you, Veeru Dada, and your gang. Now you can't escape from us," SP Vikram yelled. "Your gang is already under our custody and you are under arrest."

"It's all your doing kid, I know. No jail can keep me for a long period. Let me be out and I will emerge stronger and will pay back appropriately for your treatment of me."

The SP punched the Don with his knee and said, "You are caught badly, yet so much daring to challenge and insult the judicial system! I will see to it that you won't escape from the prison."

The police officer pushed him through the steps and brought him to the room. A few policemen were in the room with some of the gangsters.

"He is Veeru Dada, the gang leader. Take him also to the van. Be extremely careful, don't allow any of his gang to escape," the SP warned his police force.

"Let me take your leave sir," Super Kid whispered in SP's ears and disappeared from his sight immediately.

The police *captured* every one of the gang and all headed towards the police station.

35

Super Kid's noble mission to continue

Vincent sir and his two children, Jim and Jane, moved into their own house along with Uncle Sam, the faithful driver. A great sorrow still remained in the family. The children missed their most beloved and affectionate mother and Vincent sir could not pass a single moment without thinking about his dearest wife. Uncle Sam grieved for his dear mistress, Annie madam.

The staff and the workers of 'Trinity enterprises,' were extremely happy as their dear sir had come back and taken the company's reign again in his own hands. He treated them not as his subordinates or workers, but as members of his own family. They were paid well and were given all facilities. Stephen had dealt with them quite harshly and had paid also very less. No facilities were provided. They were extremely unhappy under him.

Vincent sir, with the help of Victor, got the power of attorney cancelled which Stephen had been using to sign the documents.

The families of Vincent sir and Victor met very often and they enjoyed the gatherings. They used to go for outings, picnics, parties, movies and tours.

Iqbal sir and his family were overjoyed to hear about Jim and about his reunion with his family. Same was the case of the benevolent and talented principal, Mrs. Susan, who knew Jim well and the events in his family. Both of them visited Jim's family.

Iqbal sir embraced Jim and told Vincent sir, "You are blessed to have such a son. I owe my life to him and you know his noble blood is also running through me. So I have a blood relation with him, he's also my son."

"You have already paid for his help by giving him and Jane free education in your prestigious and most well known school, "Vincent sir said quite humbly.

"That's nothing in comparison with what he has done for me. I and my family are indebted to him throughout our lives. Allow me to sponsor all his further studies."

"That's too kind of you, sir, but I feel it's not required."

"Don't tell me 'no', Mr. Vincent. Our family will be hurt deeply. It's our desire."

"Okay sir, I understand your feelings." Vincent sir had to agree.

"He's an exceptionally brilliant child. He had even made a machine named, 'Handy friend' which is extremely useful. We are using the machine in the school. Besides, he's also very helpful," the principal Mrs. Susan said and patted Jim affectionately.

They spent some time with the family and shared their happiness.

All the criminals were now put behind the bars. Victor started studying the case about Stephen, Chakrapani and Veeru Dada in detail and collected all necessary proofs. Super Kid had already given him the recording of the confession made by Veeru Dada about his own crimes as well as those of Stephen. Stephen's wife, Clara's, involvement in the murder was very evident now. He also had collected evidence to prove her involvement in drug trafficking.

While Stephen and his wife remained in the prison waiting for their trial and punishment, their only son, John, was punished by the *Juvenile court* and he was kept in the correction home, along with his friend, Raju, for their involvement in dealing with drugs, fighting with other children and other various criminal activities. They were to remain in the correction home for three years. John's example proved how a youngster could be spoiled by the parents who are themselves involved in criminal activities and who had no time to correct their son's evil ways.

Veeru Dada, Chakrapani and their gang, confined in the jail, were also waiting for their trial and judgment. A number of criminal cases including murder, drug trafficking, kidnapping were framed against them and their escape or fleeing from the jail appeared to be next to impossible. Court procedure was going to take much time. Meanwhile the criminals kept on nurturing ways and means to escape as they know that there are corrupt policemen and politicians to help them!

SP Vikram was much praised by his superiors and by the media for his success in nabbing the dreaded criminals. One day Savitri found her husband sitting lost in thought. She enquired him what was worrying him. He told her, "I have succeeded in capturing the criminals with the help of my police force, but it was mainly because of the help I got from Super Kid. Of course, only we two know about Super Kid's share. As I got his help, I doubt whether I deserve the awards and praises."

"Certainly you deserve them, because though you got Super Kid's help, he left it wisely for you to nab the criminals. Using his powers he could have brought them to the jail by himself without the help of any police. Besides, without his help, you had succeeded in several operations in the past and that's why the DGP had entrusted you with this dangerous mission."

Savitri's words removed his apprehensions and now he felt happy.

Jim was in his room alone and wished to meet Angel Shalom and suddenly she appeared in front of him. She smiled and patted him affectionately.

The Holy Messenger told him, "God is pleased with your devotion and the way you helped the needy people. You haven't misused your divine power for any personal gain. You haven't taken revenge on your enemies, but left if for the law to take its own course. God is pleased with you and He desires that you must continue the noble mission of helping those who are in distress and busting criminal activities. Now it's time for me to bid you bye. May God be with you!"

After blessing him, the Angel vanished.

Every one kept on speaking about Super Kid. The criminals shuddered at the thought of his baton whereas the upright ones and those in distress longed for his help.

Jim never disclosed his true identity to anyone but he knew that as Super Kid, he had no rest but will have to bust many more crimes and help many more people who are in distress. His noble mission has to continue!

****

Chapter Wise Word Meanings

Chapter 1

Glimpse = quick look
Gazed = looked with fixed eyes
Engulfed = covered completely
Melodious = pleasing
Herald = a person who carries an important message
Tranquility = quiet and peaceful
Rooster = an adult male chicken; cock
Engrossed = lost in complete attention
Serenity = calmness
Hawkers = people who travel about to sell their wares
Chorus = an utterance produced at the same time by a group
Marred = spoiled
Benumbed = made numb
Briskly = fast
Tormented = made to feel extreme mental pain
Prodigy = unusually talented child
Stunned = astonished
Scorn = expression of contempt or strong dislike
Lamenting = expressing grief or sadness
Sibling = a person's brother or sister
Bluntly = express something in a very direct way that may upset some people
Resentfully = feeling bitter
Slammed = shut loudly
Chaffing = teasing
Jostling = running against and shaking
Immersed = involved oneself deeply

Routine = habitual method
Forged = produced a copy of some documents for deception
Consequently = because of the reason given
Vengeance = revenge
Wardrobe = a tall piece of furniture where clothes are stored
Torture = extreme mental distress or suffering
Conspire = plan secretly to carry out some harmful or illegal act
Scare = a sudden attack of fear
Thunderstruck = extremely surprised
Consoled = gave moral or emotional strength
Siesta = afternoon nap or rest
Resolute = firm in purpose or belief
Scorching = burning
Exhausted = tired out completely
Cherish = be fond of
Nooks and cronies = every part of something
Supreme = greatest in status or authority or power
Myriad = large infinite in number
Crispy = dry and hard
Awe = an overwhelming feeling of fear, wonder or admiration
Scampered by = moved quickly
Soothing = having a calming effect
Presently = soon
Sparkling = shining brightly
Glittering = reflecting light in large amounts
Canopy = a roof like cover
Aroma = a strong, pleasant smell usually from food or drink; flavor
Lush = full of juice
Startled = excited by sudden surprise or alarm
Instinctively = without thinking
Stared = looked at with fixed eyes

Intoxicating = exciting extremely
Rekindled = arose again
Amazing = surprising greatly
Nocturnal = active during night
Beckoning = appear inviting
Curious = beyond the usual
Ugly = displeasing to the senses
Ragged = torn clothes
Sagging = hanging down
Wrinkled = marked by wrinkles or depressions
Sores = open skin infection
Stinking = having a foul smell
Disgusting = highly offensive
Pitiable = miserable
Profusely = done in large quantity, lavishly
Dazzling = blinding brightness
Splendour = magnificent and impressive appearance
Luster = a quality that outshines the usual brightness
Transformed = changed in appearance

Chapter 2

Awestruck = showing a feeling of great respect and fear
Distress = psychological suffering
Disguised = changed usual appearance to hide one's identity
Inherited = received property from someone who has died
Boon = a thing that is helpful or beneficial
Monetary = relating to or involving money
Trifles = something of little value
Discretion = freedom to act or judge on one's own; free will or tact
Utilize = use

Disclose = make known; reveal
Bestowed = given as a gift
Vicinity = nearby region
Tickle = feeling of soft touch on the body
Vanished = disappeared
Innumerable = countless

Chapter 3

Stab = thrust a knife or other pointed weapon into (someone) so as to wound or kill
Took to heels = began to run away
Drastic = in a way that is likely to have a strong or far reaching effect
Sobbed = cried noisily, taking in deep breaths
Perplexed = puzzled greatly
Underestimate *= estimate or consider something to be smaller or less important than it really is*
Resolution = a promise to yourself to do or not to do something
Spontaneously = done something in a natural way
Yearned = desired strongly or persistently

Chapter 4

Deliberately = consciously and intentionally
Benefactor = someone who gives money to help an organization, society or person
Jubilant= Feeling or expressing great happiness, especially because of a success
Ample = plentiful
Ambience = the atmosphere of a place
Amenities = things that make you comfortable and at ease
Tremendously = to a great extent

Boundless = *limitless*
Culprit = *a person responsible for a crime or other misdeed*

Chapter 5

Turn deaf ears = *refuse to listen*
Autism = *a condition or disorder that begins in childhood and causes behaviour that is usually centered on the self while limiting the development of social and communication skills*
Pranks = *practical jokes or mischievous acts*
Resembles = *to be similar to*
Conceal = *to hide from sight*
Outfit = *a set of clothes*

Chapter 6

Bewilderment = *confusion resulting from failure to understand*
Emulate = *try to be like someone you admire; imitate*
Looked daggers at = *glared very angrily at*
Blanket permission = *formal, written consent or permission given to an individual or entity to*
conduct an activity without requiring additional approval
Dawned = *began to be understood; started*
Extempore = *spoken or done without preparation; unprepared*
Baton = *a stick used by a policeman or by a conductor to direct an orchestra or choir*
Husky = *(of a person's voice) sounding rough and harsh*
Tauntingly = *saying insulting things to make another person angry*
Gnashed = *made a grinding sound by rubbing one's teeth together in anger*
Catering to = *providing to people with something they want or need*
Defecate = *to pass solid waste from the body*

Chapter 7

Adulterated = made poor by quality by adding inferior substance
Malpractice = improper practice
Brats = ill-mannered annoying children
Clown = someone who often tries to make other people laugh
Thrashing = beating
Grabbed = took hold of something or someone suddenly and roughly
Appalled = felt fear, shock or disgust
Yelled = screamed or shouted
Spilled = caused to flow
Plight = exposed to danger or sad condition
Desperate = without hope
Shudder = to shake with fear
Banteringly = speaking in a teasing manner
Arrogance = an insulting way of behaving
Hurled = threw something with force
Compensate = to make up for some defect

Chapter 8

Adage = an old well-known saying that expresses a general truth
Seldom = not often; rarely
Subordinate = a person in a position of less authority or power
Booty = property that has been stolen
Bluff = to deceive or cheat
At the end of one's wits = no more ideas to find out something
Exhaustion = the state of being extremely tired

Chapter 9

Studded = to a greater quantity
Stealthily = quietly in order to avoid being noticed

Pounding = *making a heavy repetitive sound*
Rustled = *made a soft, light sound because of rubbing against each other*
Obstruction = *something that blocks something else*
Grabbed = *quickly took hold of something*
Mustered = *gathered*
Flogging = *beating someone severely*
Expedition = *a journey undertaken for a specific purpose*

Chapter 10

Pacified = *caused to become calm*
Hideout = *a hiding place especially by someone who has broken the law*
Pounced = *sprang suddenly so as to catch prey*
Notorious = *well-known especially for something bad*
Despair = *losing all hope*
Optimistic = *having belief that good things will happen in the future*
Orphanage = *a home for children whose parents have died and are cared for*

Chapter 11

Panic = *extreme fear*
Resolutely = *very much determined*
Cow down = *be intimidated or made timid or fearful*
Crooks = *dishonest persons; criminals*
Reeled = *turned around*
Agony = *intense physical or mental suffering*
Lucrative = *producing a great deal of profit; profit making*
Amass = *to gather or collect such as a large amount of money*
Callous = *showing no sympathy for others; hard-hearted*

Bystander = a person who is standing near but not taking part in what is happening

Chapter 12

Sneak out = leave furtively and stealthily
Juvenile = relating to young people
Incarnate = in human form
Benevolent = showing kindness
Terror = an overwhelming feeling of fear and anxiety
Rowdies = cruel and brutal fellows

Chapter 13

Humanitarian = a person who works to make other people's lives better
Tandem = a group of two people or things that work together
Discarded = got rid of (something) as no longer useful or desirable
Tarnish = spoil the image
Excruciating = very painful

Chapter 14

Nasty = very unpleasant
Trap = a bad situation from which it is difficult to escape
Genius = very great and rare natural ability
Chloroform = a fluid that makes a person unconscious
Aptly = in a suitable manner
Lethal = extremely dangerous

Chapter 15

Apprehensive = feeling worried about something that is going to happen
Dreaded = extremely frightening

Chapter 16

Skeptical = doubting whether something is true or useful
Booster = something that improves or increases something
Severe = very great or intense
weired = very strange and unusual, unexpected or unnatural
Enchanted = seeming to be affected by magic
Nabbed = caught or arrested a criminal
Rusticate = suspend a student from an educational institute
Pleaded = requested for something
Repercussion = the consequences of an action
Nick of time = the last possible moment
Crestfallen = sad and disappointed
Henchman = someone who does unpleasant or illegal things for a powerful person
Compensate = give (someone) something to reduce the bad effect of loss, suffering or injury

Chapter 17

Isolated = separated from others things
Pillion = a seat behind the person riding a motor bike
Feat = something difficult needing a lot of skill
Coward = a person who is not brave
Buffoon = clown; joker
Betray = to be disloyal to your country or to a person
Handsomely = large in amount
Lavishly = generously
Frankly = in an honest and direct way
Disclose = to make something known publically
Arch = main
Meticulously = very careful and with great attention to every details

Vigilant = *always being very careful to notice things especially possible danger*

Chapter 18

Jeered = *made rude and mocking remarks on someone*
Pampered = *gave every attention, comfort and attention; spoilt*
Took to heels = *ran away*
Bunking = *remaining absent or playing truant from school*
Shrugged = *raised (one's shoulders) slightly and momentarily to express doubt, ignorance or indifference*
Queer = *strange; odd*
Taken aback = *to be shocked or surprised*
Apparition = *a remarkable thing that makes a sudden appearance, especially a ghost*
Stammered = *spoke with involuntary breaks and pauses*

Chapter 19

Adieu = *the act of leaving; farewell*
Hoarse = *a harsh low sound*
Turban = *a man's headdress worn chiefly by Sikhs*
Attire = *clothes, specially fine or formal ones*
Chuckled = *laughed gleefully or irritatingly*
Encounter = *to meet with a person unexpectedly*
Eliminate = *to remove or to get rid of*
Whereabouts = *the locality of a person*
Keep mum = *keep quiet*
Vagabond = *a person who wanders from place to place*
Disperse = *to send off in various directions; to scatter*
Tormented = *affected with great mental or physical suffering*

Chapter 20

Ravines = *deep narrow valleys*

Chapter 21

Immersed = involved oneself deeply in a particular activity
Leaped = made a large jump
Sputtered = spoke in a confusing way because one is upset, surprised, shocked etc.
Traitor = a person who is not royal or true to a friend
Treachery = behaviour that deceives someone who trusts you
Conglomeration = something consists of a number of different and distinct parts
Remorse = deep regret or guilt for a wrong committed

Chapter 22

Furiously = in an extremely angry manner
Trembled = shook involuntarily as a result of anxiety and fear
Flog = to beat with a stick or whip as a punishment
Episode = an event occurring as part of a sequence
Promptly = without delay
Pretending = behaving as if something is true when you know that it is not
Boisterous = noisy, energetic and cheerful

Chapter 23

Dejected = sad because of failure, loss depression etc.
Humiliated = make (someone) feel ashamed and foolish by injuring their dignity and pride
Crestfallen = sad and disappointed
Porn = sexually explicit videos
Tremendous = very large or great
Depicted = shown in a picture, photograph etc.
Appease = to make (someone) pleased or less angry
Blasphemy = great disrespect or insult shown to God

Hurricane = an extremely large, powerful and destructive storm
Wrath = extreme anger
Reverberated = continued in a series of echoes; resonated
Resumed = began again after stopping
Ransacked = wrongfully emptied or stripped of anything of value; plundered
Drag = force into some kind of situation, condition or course of action; involve

Chapter 24

Sarcastically = intent of ridiculing or taunting
Sedative = promoting calm or inducing sleep
Puzzle = a problem difficult to solve

Chapter 25

Intensify = to make stronger or more extreme
Suspicion = having or showing a cautious distrust of someone of something
Notorious = famous or well known, typically for some bad quality or deed
Turn over a new leaf = start to act or behave in a better or more responsible way
Panting = breathing with short, quick breaths
Trail = path
Hesitation = an action of pausing before saying or doing something
Bounce = to jump repeatedly up and down; to cause to rebound
Futile = having no effect or result
Surveillance = close watch kept over someone or something
Whizzed = moved quickly through the air with a whistling sound

Complied = did what you have been asked to do
Trespassing = enter someone's land without permission
Impregnable = unable to be broken into or captured

Chapter 26

Disguised = having its true character concealed with the intent of misleading
Racked = strained violently
Blabbering = talking foolishly or excessively
Dilapidated = fallen into ruin especially through neglect
Invigorating = causing (something) to become more active and lively
Exhilaration = the state of being cheerful
Hugged = put your hand around someone especially to show love; embraced

Chapter 27

Graveyard = a place where dead people are buried
Shot in the arm = something that boosts one's spirits

Chapter 28

Perturbed = caused to be worried or upset
Rubbish = nonsensical talk or writing
Fraud = the crime of using dishonest methods to take something valuable from another person

Chapter 29

Pathetically = causing feeling of sadness; miserably
Snatched = took (something) suddenly from a person often by using force

Premonition = a feeling that something is going to happen
Mute spectator = a person who watches silently without getting involved
Banteringly = speaking or addressing in a witty and teasing manner
Compunction = feeling of guilt or regret
Reluctantly = showing hesitation or unwillingness
Accomplishment = something that is achieved after a lot of effort

Chapter 30

Shrieked = made a loud, short high cry
Petulantly = irritated, grudgingly
Gnashed = bit or chewed by grinding the teeth
Therapy = a treatment that helps someone to feel better
Numb = unable to feel any sensation
Flabbergasted = shocked very much

Chapter 31

Ecstasy = a state of extreme happiness
Affectionately = with affection or warmth
Awesome = causing feelings of great admiration
Credibility = ability to be trusted or believed

Chapter 32

Sachets = small sealed packets containing a small quantity of something

Chapter 33

Wretched = very unhappy; full of misery

Strangle = squeeze the neck of (a person or animal), especially as to cause death

Etched = impressed into a surface; engraved

Chapter 34

Suppress = control and refrain from showing; not to reveal

Awkward = lacking grace

Custody = the state of being kept in a jail or prison

Captured = the act of conquering

Chapter 35

Juvenile court= a court of law responsible for the trial or legal supervision of children under a specified age